LETTERS *FROM* FAWN CREEK

Jonathan B. Coe

LETTERS *FROM* FAWN CREEK

TATE PUBLISHING
AND ENTERPRISES, LLC

Published by Tate Publishing & Enterprises, LLC
127 E. Trade Center Terrace | Mustang, Oklahoma 73064 USA
1.888.361.9473 | www.tatepublishing.com

Tate Publishing is committed to excellence in the publishing industry. The company reflects the philosophy established by the founders, based on Psalm 68:11,
"The Lord gave the word and great was the company of those who published it."

Cover design by Arjay Grecia
Interior design by Caypeeline Casas

Published in the United States of America

ISBN: 978-1-62854-203-5
1. Fiction / Christian / General
2. Religion / Christian Life / General
13.11.11

DEDICATION

To Brooke, Jonathan, David, and Daniel

CHAPTER 1

It took more than just a few phone calls to find my uncle's phone number and address. I didn't hire a detective to find Aaron Joiner, my mother's older brother, but, after spending all day on the phone one Saturday, I concluded that that may not have been a bad idea. Finally, Uncle Aaron's good friend Jack Arlington gave me the information. He said, "I just got off the phone with your uncle. You are dear to his heart and he has agreed to give you his address and a number he can be reached at if you promise not to give this information out to anyone else." I agreed.

Uncle Aaron used to be Pastor Aaron Joiner, senior pastor at one of the biggest churches in town, popular conference and seminar speaker, and best-selling author with three books on the non-fiction New York Times Bestseller List. These three books put him in the national spotlight. In fact, no author of non-fiction books, whether religious or secular, sold more books in a certain five year period (2004–2008) than my uncle. He wrote with both clarity and brio on the Christian life and reached a large audience across denominational lines.

Five years after his last book was published, he had all but disappeared. His whereabouts was known only to a few close family members and friends. What caused his withdrawal from public life was a series of personal tragedies and setbacks. These tribulations stood in dramatic contrast to the first twenty years of his pastorate which one friend described as "an almost unbroken series of successes." An elder in the church said, "He taught us masterfully from the Book of Job in recent years and now the Book of Job has happened to him." A professor of literature in the congregation said that Uncle Aaron's life "had become like Kafka writ large." But, instead of being arrested for no apparent reason like the protagonist in *The Trial*, my uncle had been arrested by life itself and had suffered a reversal of fortune in the realms of family, finance, and health.

One week after Uncle Aaron was named by *Time* magazine as one of the top 100 most influential people in America, his wife, Claire, and son, Jeremy, were killed in an automobile accident. He took a sabbatical from the pastorate, but before he was even halfway through his grieving process, he contracted chronic fatigue syndrome. This rendered him house-bound most of the time. He resigned from the pastorate and was replaced by the very capable and charismatic Darnelle Jackson. One year later, to make the tragic trifecta complete, he discovered that most of his financial investments were tied to a complicated Ponzi scheme. His chief investor and two associates were arrested. Uncle Aaron sold his house and disappeared.

In the years that followed, rumors about him multiplied. Some said he had lost his faith and become an alcoholic. He remarried and was living in Europe. He converted to Roman Catholicism and was studying for the priesthood. He was writing best sellers under a pseudonym. All this confirmed the observation often attributed to Mark Twain that "A lie can get halfway around the world before the truth can get its boots on…."

Uncle Aaron and I lived in the same town (before he disappeared), but while he lived out the Book of Job, I was worshipping my own trinity—wine, women, and song. Born into an evangelical Christian family of three boys and one girl, I was the wayward son who had dismissed his childhood faith as "just one religion among many" by my junior year in high school. My father asked Uncle Aaron to pray for me. He said "Carson is an experimental personality. If he hasn't tried it, it hasn't been invented yet." But every prodigal son knows one thing deep down: If you have a praying grandmother, you don't have a chance. I did have such a grandmother and began to take a second look at the religion of my youth during my senior year in college.

No doubt this second look was precipitated by a gnawing feeling of emptiness. To many scoffers and skeptics this sounds like just another religious cliché: Young man feels spiritual and emotional vacuum and looks to religion to fill it. But one must remember that stereotypes often become stereotypes because they are at least partly true. Clichés, in a different way, often become clichés because they are common, universal experiences that should not be easily dismissed.

As someone who majored in history and minored in philosophy, I began to find certain philosophical arguments compelling. The Big Bang Theory indicated that the universe in all its complexity and grandeur essentially emerged out of nothing. Something cannot emerge out of nothing. Something or someone had to cause it. This Cause had to be bigger than the universe and points to an infinite God. The parallels to the creation story in Genesis 1 and 2 were not lost on me.

It also made sense to me that this Cause that created the universe was personal and not impersonal. We live in a world full of such things as beauty, goodness, truth, love, and morality. It was more compelling to me that these qualities emerged from a God of beauty, goodness, truth, love, and morality rather than arising from mere matter in some primordial swamp.

During my search, I had an almost inevitable collision with two great minds: C. S. Lewis and Fyodor Dostoyevsky. Lewis made Christianity a reasonable faith while Dostoyevsky, especially in his great novel *The Brothers Karamazov*, adorned the gospel in a more existential and suprarational way. Later, I would say that Lewis helped convert the left side of my brain and Dostoyevsky the right. A bird after all needs two wings to fly.

Almost every conversion has a significant measure of mystery and mine was no exception. Before spring break of my senior year, I was not a Christian. After spring break, I was and, to this day, cannot explain with great specificity or linear logic what happened. As Jesus said in John 3:8: "The wind blows where it wills, and you can hear the sound it makes, but you do not know where it comes from or where it goes; so it is with everyone who is born of the Spirit."

After graduation, I took a year off. I worked long hours for my cousin painting and hanging wallpaper. I saved my money and then traveled extensively throughout Europe and Asia. I read the Bible from cover to cover and spiritual classics such as Augustine's *Confessions* and *The Imitation of Christ* by Thomas à Kempis. The ancient cathedrals and churches throughout Europe provided wonderful venues for prayer and meditation. Though I pursued silence and solitude in my travels, luminous Christians—I'm convinced by divine appointment—found me anyway, and our conversations, mostly in outdoor cafes, fell like manna from heaven. I came back home spiritually fortified and ready to launch out in new directions.

The university where I did my undergraduate work accepted me into their respected master's program in history. I began to attend the church Uncle Aaron used to pastor but then decided I could be more of an asset at a smaller, struggling community church near campus. Because I'm an experimental personality, I started an interdenominational men's Bible study for the grad students on campus. After six weeks, we had six men in regular attendance: three evangelical Protestants (including myself), two Roman Catholics, and one person who is Eastern Orthodox.

Almost from the beginning, Keith Dunston, an evangelical and doctoral candidate in philosophy, became our de facto study leader. As an ecumenical personality with a seminary degree, Keith was familiar with and respected other Christian traditions. He deftly facilitated the study with probing questions, humor, and rare insights into the "mere Christianity" that unites us all altogether. If the discussion became too intellectual and abstract, he would make a seamless segue to how the topic related to the shoe-leather of everyday life. His group discussion instincts were finely tuned. An acquaintance in the campus bookstore told me he had been in at least half a dozen discussion groups since high school and Keith was the best discussion leader he had ever seen. Everyone liked Keith and I joked that he was the kind of guy parents want their daughter to bring home—a handsome, future son-in-law. For my part, as a new believer, I was happy to start the group, but didn't want to lead it, and saw Keith as a literal godsend.

After the Bible study was eight months old, after a grueling week of exams and papers in May, I finally sat down and wrote Uncle Aaron this letter:

> Dear Uncle Aaron,
>
> How fortunate I feel to have your address and phone number and know you're alive! I solemnly promise not to give this information out to anyone and to protect your privacy. It's been three years since you sold your house and left town. Please fill me in on everything significant that has happened in your life. What's it like where you live? It sounds isolated and woodsy with lumberjacks plying their trade and logging trucks barreling down narrow country roads. Perhaps I read too much into your mailing address. I pray that you are fighting the good

fight with your illness and that God's strength is being made perfect in your weakness.

Jack Arlington told me you rejoiced because of my conversion. A former drinking buddy told me it was more likely that the Cubs would win the World Series than I would get religion. Who says miracles ended with the New Testament church?

Eight months ago, I started an interdenominational men's Bible study for grad students on campus. We had six men in regular attendance: three evangelical Protestants, two Catholics, and one Eastern Orthodox believer. As much joy as I've experienced in the last two years as a new believer, I now, with the remaining members of the study group, find myself in a season of disappointment, emotional pain, and confusion. One week ago, it came to light that our articulate and engaging study leader had a secret life that involved drug use and prostitutes. He is hiding out and cannot be reached but told me in a brief phone conversation that he is "very sorry to the group who trusted him" and "is seeking professional help for his addictions." His fiancée promptly cancelled their August wedding and has ended the relationship for good.

There's no doubt we unwisely had our study leader (Keith) on a pedestal. I think the group has, along with Keith's pastor, reached out in a compassionate and conciliatory manner. There's not much you can do when someone is in hiding. Our message has been clear to him: "We're here for you. We don't condemn you. All of us are just a step or two away from the same sins. Except for the grace of God there go I."

Keith's debacle has sent a chill through the group. The fear and trembling is palpable, because if something like this can happen to Keith, who appeared to be the paragon of Christian maturity, then what could befall us? And this now brings me to the reason for writing to you: it sure would be great to get some wise counsel from you, a seasoned veteran of the vicissitudes of life. The other guys in the study group don't know who you are. I plan to keep your identity anonymous but I did tell them—Dennis, Greg, Paul, Bill, and Alan—that I have an uncle that could help us through a difficult time.

Perhaps an analogy from history can show you how you can help us. I love nineteenth century American history, especially the movement and dynamism involved in westward expansion. The men in the study group are like immigrants from Europe who, with much risk and little money, left their homeland for the United States. Many arrived in Boston and New York. Some settled there while other more restless souls continued to move west. A small percentage of these immigrants were drawn to mining gold and silver in places like California, Nevada, and Alaska. A smaller percentage still actually struck it rich in mining. Many went broke trying.

In translating the analogy to spiritual terms, the immigrants leaving their homeland are like a people's initial conversion when they believe they have left all things for Christ. Striking gold at Sutter's Mill or on the Klondike is like, after your life is over, hearing Christ say to you: "Well done, you good and faithful servant." In between these two experiences—leaving our homeland and striking gold—the journey is fraught with suffering and glory, blessings and curses, consolation and desolation, risk and reward. Keith, because of his own foolishness, on his journey to the gold rush, has been attacked and seriously wounded by a grizzly bear in Devil's Canyon. I earnestly pray for his full recovery.

In between these two experiences, it is most helpful to have an experienced guide across the plains, mountains, deserts, and forests who knows both the landscape and dangers and also where to look to find the gold. With all that you've been through in recent years, I don't want to add another burden to what you've already carried. The group doesn't need you to write another book—a couple of brief letters of distilled avuncular wisdom should do.

Grace and peace to you.

In Christ,
Carson

It should be obvious to the reader that, while we didn't ask for a book, we got one anyway. Dennis, who is almost finished with a master's program in economics, called the letters "Screwtape in Reverse." In *The Screwtape Letters*, the elder devil Uncle Screwtape tutors his nephew Wormwood on how to, by demonic manipulation, destroy men's souls. In the book you hold in your hands, Uncle Aaron graciously tries to lead us through gates of splendor to a spiritual Klondike, to the throne of Christ, and to the words we all want to hear: "Well done, you good and faithful servant."

CHAPTER 2

Dear Carson,

What a delight to hear from you and learn about what has happened in your life the last two years! God has certainly heard the prayers of Grandma Lois, your parents, and my own efforts, however imperfect, to pray for you. When I heard about your conversion, I danced a little jig, shouted for joy to heaven, and hoisted a glass of good pale ale that evening in your honor.

Like you, I regret that the occasion of your letter—the exposure of your study group leader—had to be so emotionally devastating for all parties involved. I'll comment on this matter later in the letter but, for now, it is enough to say that your humble and compassionate outreach to Keith is laudable. Remember this too: He who is forgiven much loves much. Keith could emerge from this like Mary Magdalene—humble, grateful, and much more in love with Jesus than your "average sinner" because he has been forgiven much. Let's intercede to that end and be sure to enlist Grandma Lois too in praying for the fallen young man.

You had some questions about my recent history. Much has been written and spoken about me becoming a recluse. With all that happened, initially I simply wanted to be alone with my grief and my "Golgotha friends." I call them Golgotha friends because they were there with me through the most emotionally and spiritually excruciating season of my life. Men, more often than women, go through these experiences without such friends or end up with a company of Job's "sorry comforters." They've placed achievements far above relationships, and then, in a time of personal crisis, have a master's degree and a six-figure salary but no intimate friends. Others kept their relationships safe without much vulnerability and so there was no emotional mortar to build intimacy. Some were simply too busy and didn't have the time to get to know them.

I made all of these mistakes until I was about thirty-seven years old. Claire was my only Golgotha friend. But his mercies endure forever and, as I sit here writing this, I have at least a half a dozen such people I can get real with. They've seen me at my worst, warts and all, and have not abandoned me.

As you know, rumors about me have multiplied like rabbits. This actually drove me further into a solitary existence. I've considered giving a brief phone interview with a good and trusted journalist like John Rader to put to rest a lot of the hearsay. I think of a famous saying from Rabbi Hillel in the *Mishnah*: "If I am not for myself, who will be for me? Yet, if I am for myself only, what am I? And if not now, when?"

The rumors are not entirely false. I did not lose my faith and become an alcoholic. I did, however, have an autumn when I first moved to the cabin when I simply drank too much. I became reacquainted with an old friend named "Glen" (Glenfiddich Single Malt Scotch

Whisky) that I first met while studying abroad as an undergrad in Scotland my senior year. I wish I could say I sobered up because of some lofty reason like wanting to obey and honor God. I didn't. Don't get me wrong; personal growth can be a noble aspiration but it can be tainted by narcissism. During summer several years ago, I preached at a handful of churches in the West Coast at the end of a long speaking tour. Many in the audience were from the baby-boomer generation and seemed to have an inordinate preoccupation with finding their gifts and ministries. They also seemed overly concerned with whether they were growing fast enough spiritually.

These were all biblical Christians, but I sensed life was still too much about them. It felt as if some of the narcissism of the 1960s and 1970s, the decades where they came of age, had been transferred into the church and was dressed up in religious language. As I was making this assessment, I realized I had been, to a smaller degree, bitten by the same bug!

The great Christian mystic Jean-Pierre de Caussade lauds the virtue of self-forgetfulness in his timeless classic *Abandonment to Divine Providence*. It is the antidote for religious narcissism. Certain practices have really helped me to move outward and stay other-centered: counting my blessings, intercessory prayer, helping someone less fortunate, etc. We all need certain disciplines we can do to counteract the gravity-pull of self-centeredness.

Now, getting back to the issue of addictions and personal growth. A second cousin of mine who is now a chemical dependency counselor drank heavily from age 18 to 38. When he got clean and sober, he had to deal with the fact that he had the emotional maturity of an 18 year old. Addictions push the pause button on many areas of personal growth. I fear this stagnation as much as I fear serial killers who dress up as clowns. When you watch a really bad movie, that's two hours you can't get back. Well, I have two months with Glenfiddich I can't get back, and yet, in some mysterious way, I know that God can work redemptively in my failures.

For example, after I poured what was left of "Glen" down the drain, I used the cabin to go on a seven-day retreat in order to clear my head and reconnect with God. It was a rather dreary and uneventful time that left me asking: "Where is the God of Elijah?" I thought I heard God reply: "Where are the Elijahs?" However, while walking to the mailbox about a week later, I heard this deep in the inner recesses of my being: "I'm leading you out of a public pastoral ministry to a ministry of contemplative and intercessory prayer, writing, and encouraging church leadership."

Since then, I've been practicing these four things. The writing hasn't been best sellers but has instead been personal letters and I'm content with that. About every other month, a church leader will come for a visit and some even stay for a full week. They usually leave refreshed with a new spring in their step, not, I'm convinced, because of me but in spite of me. We do pray together and I always try to encourage them by affirming the goodness and giftedness in each person. It's definitely not a ministry where I utter profound insights to the leader and they then go back to their ministries ready to conquer the world. It's more of a ministry of me getting out of the way and letting God speak to them in a significant way, often in an unspectacular way after they leave Fawn Creek.

One rumor is that I converted to Roman Catholicism and am studying for the priesthood. That's half true. I did become a Catholic just one month ago on Easter. After much prayer and study of the early church fathers, I became convinced that the early church looked an awful lot like the Catholic Church. This shocked some friends and family members but I've emerged from the experience with the same profound love and respect I had before for different streams—Catholic, Protestant, and Orthodox—that feed the river of God. As your study group receives letters from me from now on, I can only promise to try to do what Keith did at his best: Keep his own religious convictions in a healthy tension with the "mere Christianity" that unites us.

The outpouring of concern about my chronic fatigue syndrome (CFS) from many people has warmed my heart. It could be so much worse. Some sufferers of CFS are completely bedridden and unable to care for themselves. I can care for myself though it's wise for me to stay at home most of the time. Some wonderful people from my church (St. Matthew's) deliver groceries and supplies to the cabin occasionally and a handyman from the same parish fixed a plumbing problem I had. Christ had his Passion and I know this is a part of mine. However, I still complain to God about the persistent fatigue not relieved by sleep, the headaches, the pain in joints, and the chills and night sweats.

Recently, I jokingly asked God: "Why me? Why can't there be an equal distribution of misery like some countries try to equally distribute wealth?" Then I have my good days when I embrace what Catholics call "offering it up," a practice that unites our cross to his cross and has redemptive purposes for both the believer and unbeliever.

You asked about the region where I live. First, I am so thankful to be here. While I was trying to sell my house, a wealthy parishioner of the church I used to pastor mentioned he had a vacation cabin in northeast Washington State near the Canadian border. As a widower in his early eighties, he doesn't use the cabin anymore and offered to set up a house-sitting arrangement with me. His only child lives in Europe and hasn't been to the place in five years. Despite suffering significant financial loss because of my investor's Ponzi scheme, I still have enough revenue coming in to cover my basic needs and pay a little rent. The owner, Rick Longstreet, refuses rent money and says he's just happy someone's making use of the cabin that was very dear to his late wife Sally. The money set aside for rent now goes to the poor.

The cabin is not upscale but it is not spartan either. It has all the amenities—running water, electricity, a flush toilet—in a three-bedroom, one-bathroom home of 1100 square feet that is both quaint and rustic. The gambrel roof with its barn-like design makes it quaint, while the stained exterior siding and the stained and varnished interior knotty pine paneling make it rustic. A large wood stove provides the main source of heat during the cold months and is supplemented by electric baseboard heat.

What struck me most about my first month at Fawn Creek—a.k.a God's country—was how such an idyllic setting was juxtaposed with my turbulent personal life. One hundred miles north of Spokane, you find yourself in some of the densest forests in eastern Washington. You drive down a gravel road lined with cedar and huckleberry bushes that eventually open up to a verdant valley with Fawn Creek running through it. Wheeler Mountain serves both as a backdrop and some say as a 5,000-foot "sentinel" guarding the valley from "bad spirits." The cabin itself sits on a knoll overlooking the creek with small meadows on either side. I've caught pan-sized rainbow and cutthroat trout just fifty feet away from my back door. I don't fish Fawn Creek too heavily. I don't want to deplete the already small trout population and try to leave some fish for the kids in the valley.

You mentioned that my mailing address sounded "isolated and woodsy with lumberjacks plying their trade and logging trucks barreling down narrow country roads." Before I even left for Fawn Creek, Rick Longstreet jokingly told me, "It may take you awhile to get used to the isolation. The closest town is Conner's Point and it's fifteen miles away and only has a population of 250 people. It's a one-horse town and the horse died!"

The lumber industry around here is actually in decline, though you do still see some logging trucks coming down out of Magee Pass. My neighbors are primarily self-reliant tradesmen but we do have some schoolteachers, entrepreneurs, one couple that work as administrators in the Forest Service, and a sprinkling of retired folk. I drive thirty miles one way to attend mass at St. Matthew's in Clayton, a town of 7,500 that has everything you need and serves a population within a thirty-mile radius of the town.

What an honor and delight to be asked by your study group to pass on a little wisdom this feeble servant of God has slowly acquired over the years. This isn't false humility. Using your analogy of the American West and the pursuit of gold and silver (striking gold equals hearing "Well done, you good and faithful servant"), much of my authority to offer counsel is because I've spent a lot of time in places like "Starvation Valley," fighting off wild animals and bandits in a hot, arid wilderness. "Travel guides" such as Pride and Vanity led me to such wastelands; Mercy and Grace led me out.

It should also be emphasized that nothing I say in the forthcoming letters is new. In fact, I would be disappointed if anyone in your study group called me an "original thinker." Much of what I write is as old as the Garden of Eden and has been already covered by the biblical authors and the luminous figures that grace the pages of centuries of church history. To preach the kingdom of God today is to take ancient truth and communicate it in a fresh, clear, and engaging manner. Unfortunately, novelty seems to be the *sine qua non* of much modern and post-modern theology and leads people away from the ancient paths.

Hearing about the debacle of your former study leader Keith made me think of a prayer breakfast I attended during the early years of my pastorate. About a week before the breakfast, it came out that a co-founder of a successful campus ministry in town was resigning from the ministry because it was discovered that he had embezzled tens of thousands of dollars from the organization's coffers over several years. The incident was discussed by many ministers around me before and after the prayer time. It wasn't until years later that I understood the significance of the variety of responses.

The young bucks were aghast, the middle-aged ministers were somewhat surprised, and the senior pastors, the hoary heads, showed little or no astonishment. I asked a retired pastor, Bob Bonelli, who was at the time serving as an interim pastor in a suburban church, why he wasn't surprised. Without hesitating, he said, "Because I know how weak people are and how weak I am." This truth was lost on the young pastors while it had been, over the years, inscribed in Bob's heart and mind by watching people fall and by being acutely aware of the fragility of his own soul.

Since I haven't spent any time with them, I don't know the hearts of the men (Dennis, Paul, Bill, Greg, and Alan) in your study group and only offer some general observations concerning their response to Keith's fall. First, if the incident sent a chill through the group, I say "Good!" Tradition suggests that St. Francis of

Assisi said the only thing we should fear is sin. The group's reaction reveals a fear of sin rooted in a healthy reverence for God.

In order for this fear not to become paralyzing, it needs to be counterbalanced by a restful trust that Christ living through you ("Christ in you, your *only* hope of glory") will gradually lead you to the Yukon gold strike. Remember it is faith and not self-effort that is inextricably linked to Christian growth:

> For the love of God is this, that we keep his commandments. And his commandments are not burdensome, for whoever is begotten by God conquers the world. And the victory that conquers the world is our *faith* [emphasis mine]. Who [indeed] is the victor over the world but the one who believes that Jesus is the Son of God?
>
> I John 5:3–5

Again, I don't know the hearts of the men in your group but I suspect at least one of them was like me at that prayer breakfast years ago and didn't have an awareness of how weak human beings really are. This results in at least part of the astonishment that says, "How could Keith do this?!" However, if you want to make it to that rich silver strike in Tonopah, Nevada, it starts with this awareness—it starts with humility.

Humility is not groveling. Humility is an objective evaluation of yourself and the situation you find yourself in. Perhaps an exaggerated illustration would help. Biblical wisdom tells us that humanity is below the angels but above the animals on the earth's chain of being. If we say we are like the angels and will easily make it to Tonopah, Nevada, for the silver strike, we are not humble; we are proud. But if we say that we are no better than the animals and have no chance of making it to Tonopah, we're not humble either. We're probably practicing a false humility. Only when we say that we are above the beasts but below the angels, and that only a radical dependence on the grace (ability) of God will get us to the silver strike, only then are we humble. We are humble because we speak the truth: Humility is truth; truth is humility. Only then does our life begin to resonate with the heart of Jesus, meek and lowly: "I am the vine, you are the branches. Whoever remains in me and I in him will bear much fruit, because without me you can do nothing." (John 15:5)

Think of yourself as a young man growing up in Europe in the nineteenth century. You are frail and sickly and come from one of the wealthiest aristocratic families in the country. You grow up in a socioeconomic cocoon that both pampers you and insulates you from hard work and what common folk call "the real world."

An older man and adventurer that you respect returns from his year in America and regales you with splendid food, spirits, stories about the American West and the gold and silver mining that is going on there. Feeling both stultified by the aristocratic subculture you inhabit and possessed by the wanderlust of youth, you ask your father to bankroll an adventure to look for gold with the older man in northern California. At first your father says no but then reasons that: "Time abroad would be good for you. It would make you a man of the world and perhaps force you to grow up."

In many ways, the young man is the most unlikely candidate for a successful adventure. He has significant physical limitations and his upbringing has not prepared him for the obstacles he will face in the coming year. At the same time, he has a willing heart and seemingly unlimited financial resources to make it happen. He has the money to pay for the expensive medicine that helps him physically. He can foot the bill for the older man and take the best boat for the trip across the Atlantic. When he arrives in New York, he can purchase any goods and/or services he needs to make the trip to California successful, and once there, hire the best prospectors to find the gold.

We are like this young man. We are very weak ("… without me you can do nothing") but we have access to plentiful and amazing resources because "His divine power has bestowed on us everything that makes for life and devotion, through the knowledge of him who called us by his own glory and power" (2 Peter 1:3). Whether Roman Catholic, Protestant, or Eastern Orthodox, we need to know that these "plentiful and amazing resources" are not abstract concepts but is a person living through us, the Lord Jesus Christ. Remember, to gain a supernatural end you must have a supernatural means to achieve it. You want to know Christ intimately, be conformed to his image, and hear him say "Well done, you good and faithful servant," but nothing less than a radical dependence on Christ living through you can achieve this.

It took me years to learn these simple truths. The verbally nimble have both a great gift and a great temptation. Excellent communication skills and deft diplomacy can bring success but also can insulate us from the truth of how weak we really are. In the early years of my pastorate, I learned that I could talk people into things. The church needs to become more seeker-sensitive? I'll talk them into it. The church needs both a traditional and a contemporary service? I'll talk them into it. It reminds me of what a certain Chinese Christian said after speaking at several churches in America: "It's amazing what the American church can accomplish without the help of the Holy Spirit."

My early successes created a hubris that dulled my awareness about just how pathetic I was without God. Then the best thing happened to me that could happen—a colossal failure. As I saw churches in my denomination being renewed by the charismatic dimension, I thought I could bring the factions together in our church by, again, talking them into it. Instead, we had a "backdoor revival" and lost 20% of our members! I was crestfallen. For the first time in my life, I couldn't get people to do what I wanted through words and diplomacy. The failure, however, was redemptive in moving me closer to biblical humility. The congregation also recovered and experienced a new vitality in the years that followed.

In his biography, *The Life of St. Anthony the Great,* St. Athanasius describes the many temptations by the devil St. Anthony suffered while he lived in the desert of Egypt in the third and fourth centuries. He saw a world full of the snares and traps around him and cried out for deliverance to God. He then heard a voice that told him, "Humility shall escape them without more."

A humble person is like a boxer who has developed an excellent defensive strategy. After a few frustrating rounds, his opponent returns to his corner and tells everyone around him: "I can't get a good, clean shot on this guy. Fighting this guy is like drinking coffee with a fork."

This is what happened in the famous fight between Muhammad Ali and George Foreman in 1974. Ali employed the rope-a-dope defensive strategy and Foreman couldn't land any significant blows. After seven rounds, Foreman had exhausted himself and went down in a heap as Ali became the aggressor in round eight. Resist the devil with humility and he will flee in defeat.

On the road to a Nevada silver strike, the adventurer will encounter many obstacles, some external and some internal. Externally, he may have to face difficult terrain, bad weather, bandits, unfriendly Indians, scarcity of water, wild animals, etc. Internally, he may have to face his own characters flaws: impatience, lack of fortitude, and/or not being a team player.

On our pilgrimage in this life, we will battle three enemies: the world, the flesh, and the devil. Two are external, one is internal. The world is anything on the earth that is opposed to God and his ways. The devil is the ruler of this world (2 Corinthians 4:4) and is completely opposed to God and his ways. The flesh is anything *within* us that is opposed to God and his ways.

Without humility, we are easy prey for the world, the flesh, and the devil. We become Satan's chew toy, his plaything. If this letter should make even just a modicum of sense to the members of your study group, I leave you all with these two words: "Get small!"

I must close now and get ready for a friend who is coming over in an hour. He is the senior priest at my church and is stopping by for beer and cigars. After that, we are going walleye fishing on the Columbia River at dusk on a sandy beach near the Canadian border. With CFS, I may regret this tomorrow, but the prospect of both good friendship and good fishing is difficult to pass up.

My prayers are with you and the study group.

Under the Tender Mercies,
Uncle Aaron

Dear Carson,

After I mailed my letter to you, I realized that I had forgotten to give you the rules Mother Teresa had given the sisters under her care (the Missionaries of Charity) to live by to cultivate the virtue of humility. These rules took me five minutes to read, but will take me the rest of my life to live:

1. Speak as little as possible about yourself.
2. Keep busy with your own affairs and not those of others.
3. Avoid curiosity.
4. Do not interfere in the affairs of others.

5. Accept small irritations with good humor.
6. Do not dwell on the faults of others.
7. Accept censures even if unmerited.
8. Give in to the will of others.
9. Accept insults and injuries.
10. Accept contempt, being forgotten, and disregarded.
11. Accept injuries and insults.
12. Be courteous and delicate even when provoked by someone.
13. Do not seek to be admired and loved.
14. Give in, in discussions, even when you are right.
15. Always choose the more difficult task.

Since she repeats herself on some of the rules, I assume these must be the most difficult ones for us to obey. "Repetition is the mother of learning," someone once said.

Under the Tender Mercies,
Uncle Aaron

CHAPTER 3

Dear Carson,

It was a great pleasure to talk to you on the phone the other night. When my new landline was installed last week, my neighbor, Jim McAndrew, who has been my message phone since I moved to Fawn Creek, jokingly said, "Welcome to the twentieth century!" Early on I embraced the message phone arrangement because it enhanced the privacy I was pursuing and Jim, a retired auto mechanic, was so accommodating. He said it gave him an opportunity to visit me some evenings and smoke cigars, drink good nut brown ale (his favorite), and have "good Catholic fun" with me.

Recently, I told him I was grateful to smoke cigars many evenings now that the non-winter months are here. He joked, "Non-winter months? You mean June and July?" He exaggerates, of course, but Fawn Creek does seem to be a magnet for all the inclement weather in the county. Winter comes earlier here and stays longer than Conner's Point which is only fifteen miles away.

I had to laugh at your reaction to the rules Mother Teresa gave the sisters under her care: "Woe is me!" Don't feel too bad; I've broken all these rules many times in my life and, if I was a woman, would've lasted about three days with the Missionaries of Charity.

Your phone call caused me to ruminate over many things. Because I'm going through a rough stretch with my illness (yes, the outing walleye fishing with Father Hewitt didn't help but it was worth it. The Columbia River was sublime and gave up her bounty—three keepers with one weighing four pounds!), it would be wise to take it one issue at a time and not try to cover everything in one letter.

You may be giving me too much credit by saying that my honesty over my failures in my letter coupled with Keith's fall has caused the members of your study group to confess their struggles—anger, lust, overeating, selfish ambition, jealousy, etc. You are right in saying that "vulnerability begets vulnerability" but you're probably overlooking what a safe place the group has created for itself without me.

One common theme that emerged in our conversation is that everyone in the group recognizes that they were delivered of many sins at conversion (or re-commitment to Christ) but some sins stubbornly endured. There also seems to be a general consensus that the religious formulas employed to overcome the post-conversion sins have failed. Many in the group have hit a wall.

A professor of pastoral theology, Dr. Riley Dixon, used to say, "Formulas don't work; God works!" Christian bookstores and today's pulpit are awash in the formulaic approach. "Read the Bible, pray, attend church services and it will be okay." Titles often have "Three Steps," "Four Keys," or "Five Ways" to some victorious outcome. My litmus test for a book or sermon is this: If it emphasizes the weakness of the human being and the necessity of a radical dependence on and a restful trust in the person of Christ, then it will probably be helpful. If it doesn't have this emphasis, then it can have a myriad of bad outcomes.

Read through some of the chapters of the Gospel of John sometime. There's a definite pattern where a crisis arises (e.g. John 2:1–2, John 11:1–44) and human resources are exhausted. They have no wine (John 2:3). Lazarus has been dead for four days and stinks (John 11:39). The awareness of our own bankruptcy leads to a brokenness and dependent turning to Christ who then comes to us as deliverer. However, if someone can work through their crisis using a formulaic approach undergirded by self-effort, it will often result in self-righteousness and a critical spirit—"If I can overcome X, then why can't you?" Fortunately, most people fail enough that they are ready to move into brokenness and dependence. If the members of the study group have hit a wall, then I say "Hallelujah!" You're in a good place.

Kierkegaard was on target when he said that anxiety is the result of human beings, who were created finite and free, confronting life's difficulties. If we were infinite like God, we would simply make the problem go away. If we were automatons and faced a crisis, there would be no anxiety because we would simply do what we were programmed to do. But since we are limited beings with free will, when we face adversity, there will be anxiety and life will feel out of control. Christians often turn to religious formulas when life feels this way.

When they can't stop at two beers, life feels out of control. When their goodnight kiss to their girlfriend goes much further than that, they feel out of control. When their volcanic anger erupts because they were passed over for a promotion, life feels out of control. Good things such as prayer, Bible study, and church attendance become formulas that promise to alleviate the anxiety and solve the problem. Unfortunately, people often become more dependent on a formula than the Father, Son, and Holy Spirit and end up disillusioned.

As a young pastor, I had more formulas than any mathematics professor at MIT. But the messiness of life experience has a way of reducing tidy categories to rubble. One of the first things I noticed in my congregation was the presence of wonderful parents who had bad kids and, conversely, bad parents who had wonderful kids. This didn't accord at all with the formulas I had about training children.

About the same time, I took my son Jeremy to his first professional baseball game when he was six. When we arrived at the ballpark, I could tell he was made a little afraid by the unfamiliar sights and sounds. Masses of people filing through the turnstiles. Loud vendors hawking beverages and hot dogs. Fans reacting wildly to instant replay of the home team's dramatic comeback win the night before.

All these things naturally put Jeremy on edge and he clung tightly to my hand as we went to find our seats. He was anxious but he put his trust completely in me to be there for him through a new experience. By the third inning, he was as comfortable as a twenty-year season-ticket holder!

Intimacy is one of God's highest kingdom priorities. He brought Israel out of Egypt so that they would become a kingdom of priests in close relationship to him (Exodus 19:6). Jesus applauded Mary for choosing to sit at his feet and listen to him and highlighted this closeness as *the one* important thing (Luke 10:38–42). God wants intimacy with his sons and daughters, and, not coincidentally, life provides fertile soil for this relationship but it also provides a context for idolatry.

The anxiety, stress, and out-of-control feeling that Kierkegaard wrote about is inherent to human existence—it cannot be eradicated this side of eternity. How we respond to this reality will determine what kind of people we become, and, to return to your mining analogy, whether we strike it rich in the Yukon or not. If we confess our own bankruptcy and cling to Christ as Jeremy clung to me at the ballgame, we will incrementally grow in closeness to God. If we don't confess our weakness but cling to something else beside Christ—even if it is religious formulas—we'll grow in idolatry. Formulas often retard intimacy.

Life is full of small, medium, and large decisions to go one way or the other. As many writers have emphasized, we *become* our decisions. A man may occasionally overeat, but, through repeated practice, he *becomes* a glutton. We become like what we cling to, whether it's an idol or Jesus of Nazareth. A young actor grows up idolizing Jack Nicholson. In time, he will resemble the screen legend in body language, countenance, and cadence of speech.

Formulas often break down when they run into life in all its complexity, absurdity, and mystery. Imagine a young Irishman sitting in a pub in Boston planning an ambitious trip out to northern California to mine gold in the 1840s. His uncle who has experience in both the journey and the mining endeavor tells him over pints of ale: "Do these five things and you will be successful." A month later the nephew makes the trip and the five bits of advice are helpful until he finds himself in the Utah desert and confronts a problem his uncle's advice doesn't address. It would've been better for the uncle to say "The five bits of advice I gave you will help you a lot but it doesn't cover everything. They don't call it the Wild West for nothing. Expect the unexpected."

Put another way, during our sojourn on earth, in our relationship with God and people, make room for mystery. Making room for mystery is a good tonic for the formulaic approach. Remember that God's ways are not your ways and his thoughts are not your thoughts (Isaiah 55:8, 9). He is infinite, we are finite. He is in heaven, we are on earth. He is *Wholly Other* and an infinite chasm exists between himself and the created order. In this gulf lies a Great Mystery.

This explains what happened when God became man in the person of Jesus Christ. Because he was Other, Christ had conflict with the religious authorities, the crowds, and the twelve disciples. Even his inner circle—Peter, James, and John—were often at odds with him. Peter took issue with Christ's first prediction of His Passion and Christ rebuked him, saying, "Get behind me, Satan! You are an obstacle to me. You are thinking not as God does, but as human beings do" (Matthew 16:23). You could never get your "sea legs" with Christ; his thoughts, words, and deeds kept everyone off balance.

When I was a student in seminary, I enjoyed exegesis papers and was good at them. You would take a passage of Scripture and mine its meaning by studying the original language (vocabulary, grammar, etc.), cultural background, historical background, contemporary scholarship, etc. I always felt satisfied after the paper was finished and part of it was because I thought I had learned something new and had a handle on some small corner of the kingdom of God. Put another way, I felt I had more control.

But one semester, in my last year, while studying the Book of Ecclesiastes, a text that tends to blow up religious formulas, I had a much different experience. One evening, at the end of writing the paper, I felt as if I had lightly brushed up against the Wholly Other God. Rather than a comfortable feeling of control, I knew it was a "fearful thing to fall into the hands of the living God" (Hebrews 10:31). Like Job, I admitted my limitations and was humbled before an incomprehensible Mystery (Job 42:1–6). All my sophisticated interpretive tools sat on my study table—the best books available—and merely seemed like a pail that a small child dips into the Pacific Ocean or an ice pick that a mountaineer uses on Mount Everest.

What's sometimes overlooked is that because people are created in the image of God, they are also "other" and are marked by an incomprehensible mystery. There is a sense in Jeremiah 17:9 that the human heart is full of twists and turns and difficult to understand and is often marked by deceit. Dostoyevsky recognized the enigma of the human condition and gave his energies to understanding it, and, as a result, provided psychological insights that were decades ahead of his time. How often do we find ourselves saying, "I can't believe he or she did that!" We wouldn't say that if we weren't rubbing shoulders with a mystery.

Returning to a major theme of my first letter, it takes humility to eschew the formulaic approach, to throw off the "burden of omniscience," and embrace the mysteries of God and people. This will at first maybe lead to a feeling of a loss of control, but will eventually result in a rest for our souls, a rest that is fertile soil for changes that occur from the inside out.

With spring run-off happening, Fawn Creek is swollen and is overflowing its banks a little here and there. The sound of the creek at night when I go to bed would make great background music for a choir of angels, a kind of transcendent exuberance ascending to the Milky Way above.

Father Hewitt tells me the rainbow trout are biting at the mouth of Mill Creek where it flows into the Columbia River. He told me to keep quiet about it. He has a secret hole. Life is about tradeoffs. What I gain spiritually, emotionally, and psychologically from these outings with the good reverend outweighs the physical toll it takes on me.

I have more to say concerning our recent phone conversation and will get back to you soon. Grace and peace be to all of you and may God strengthen you during this time of final exams and papers.

Under the Tender Mercies,
Uncle Aaron

CHAPTER 4

Dear Carson, Dennis, Greg, Paul, Bill, and Alan:

Since it sounds like everyone in the study group is reading my letters, I've addressed this letter to everyone. I hope this letter finds you, after a grueling season of exams and papers, prospering in body, soul, and spirit and growing closer to Jesus each day. I know he looks at you all with eyes of delight as each one of you takes a courageous emotional and spiritual inventory of your lives.

The mouth of Mill Creek yielded its bounty for Father Hewitt but not for me. In a gentle rain under leaden skies, he landed two eighteen-inch rainbow trout that can only be described as "outdoor magazine perfect." I use this description because they looked just like the trout you would see in an outdoor magazine hanging from the stringer of a professional fly fisherman after his outing on some blue-ribbon stream in Montana.

My experience at Mill Creek was the familiar one of the big one that got away. I did catch and release a twelve-incher and told the fish that I'd be back for him next year at this time. Then, a half an hour later, a big one hit my rod like a lead pipe. The drag screamed out of my reel as the fish danced and splashed on the water like Fred Astaire and Ginger Rogers. Father Hewitt said, "You got a two-footer on. Maybe bigger." The behemoth danced and splashed some more. I had him five feet from the shore before he made another run and snapped the line by wrapping it around a big rock.

Father Hewitt dropped the net he was holding and we both sighed in disappointment. I then pointed to him and said, "The Lord giveth," and then pointed to me and said, "The Lord taketh away." We both had a good laugh.

Father Hewitt has in some ways become my spiritual director. After the outing, over cigars and good port, he encouraged me as a new Catholic to pray the Rosary, something he's been doing for thirty years. He said to start with one decade and then to gradually add a decade here and there until I'm praying the entire prayer. Father Hewitt is a big man (250 pounds) and played linebacker in high school. With the rosary and other spiritual disciplines, he emphasized "not to try to do too much too soon. Be content with incremental growth. Don't try to bench press 300 pounds your first day in the weight room."

Due to my illness and other factors, I was unable to write a single word for an entire week after the fishing trip. Just making it to Sunday morning mass felt like a major accomplishment. I did, however, take time to reflect on our most recent phone conversation and relate it to my last letter about the importance of eschewing the formulaic approach. This is a critical juncture on the road to the gold strike in the Yukon and a word of balance is needed. As I wrote in a previous letter, there are three enemies of your soul that are opposed to God and His ways: the world, the flesh, and the devil. When an earnest, spiritually engaged Christian jettisons a formulaic approach concerning such things as prayer, Scripture study, church attendance, the sacraments, etc., these three corrosive influences will try to get that believer to quit praying, fellowshipping, confessing their sins—in short, to become spiritually disengaged.

Father Hewitt has seen his fair share of fallen priests as a life-long Catholic. With a look of sadness in his eyes, he told me that their stories almost always begin with "Father stopped praying." We are God's vineyard (Isaiah 5:1–7). Spiritual disciplines are one of the primary ways that vineyard receives photosynthesis ("Sonshine") and is watered, fertilized, and tilled. Emotional and spiritual health is inextricably linked to spiritual engagement.

What I write here is an elementary truth of the kingdom that Sunday school teachers often try to impart to the children in their classes. A pastor friend of mine of a large church in California says he has to emphasize this truth over and over to his flock because America, since the 1960s, has become a feeling-based culture. The mantra became "If it feels good, do it." Many people say they pray when the feeling comes upon them. This is just the kind of prayer life the enemy wants us to have.

Over the years, prayer has, for the most part, gone from drudgery to delight for me but I still have my feeling-based moments. My flesh—that thing within me opposed to God and his ways—recoils at the idea of prayer and I wait for a feeling. Then I remind myself that life has a semitruck-load of things that I initially don't feel like doing but still need to get done.

Many of us get up in the morning, bathe, brush our teeth, and fight traffic on the way to work. At work, we are greeted by moody co-workers, difficult projects, and stressful deadlines. We fight traffic on the way home, drop the kids off at soccer practice, and balance the checkbook before we pick the kids up and take them home. Tomorrow is trash pickup so we need to get the trash and the recycling down to the street. Finally, we get dinner and watch a little television and ask our spouse about her day. As we reflect on our day, we realize how much of it are things we, in our flesh, don't want to do. But, as we embrace the toil and the stress and even the sorrow, there is a mature satisfaction—i.e. happiness—that emerges at the end of the day that far surpasses the fun we had cracking wise at Saturday night's cocktail party. The same satisfaction exists when we resist the flesh and make the journey from prayerlessness to prayer. It is believed by many that Helen Keller opined that "True happiness…is not attained through self-gratification, but through fidelity to a worthy purpose."

When the formulaic approach is abandoned, this is often a critical juncture on the way to the silver strike. The world, the flesh, and the devil can converge in a cacophony of voices with the sole purpose being the spiritual disengagement of the Christian. It's a kind of toxic symphony; the devil is the conductor.

One false voice you're likely to hear is what I call the voice of false pragmatism. It will ask you, "Why pray, read the Bible, attend church, or participate in the sacraments? All that didn't help you with your anger problem." Again, spiritual disciplines are a means to spiritual and emotional health and serve as bridges to intimacy to God but are not a formula to solve all of life's problems in short order. Expect some protracted struggles in your life concerning diverse issues.

A second false voice that sometimes overlaps with the voice of pragmatism is the voice of offense. I have much to say on this topic and will give a more thorough treatment to it in other letters. Sometimes, Christians are hoping that because they depended on formula A, they will receive desired outcome B. If it doesn't work, they become offended at God and jettison spiritual disciplines. Why pray, read Scripture, or participate in sacraments if it doesn't work? Why try to connect with God who has offended you?

Many earnest Christians have offended hearts and are in denial about it. Their baby daughter contracts a rare disease and dies despite their fervent prayers. To confess to others that they are offended at God feels like sacrilege. In some "hyperreligious" churches, they might be considered unspiritual if they were honest with their feelings.

Their best course of action, and the one I pursued in recent years in the wake of my affliction, is to come out of denial, have it out with God, and wrestle with him as Jacob did at the river Jabbok. The key is to, like Job, not let your complaint develop into a permanent, bitter offense. God is big enough to handle our greatest fury and compassionate enough to lead us to transformative healing.

Another false voice you'll probably hear is what I call the voice of authenticity. Since our flesh will recoil at the thought of embracing spiritual disciplines, a voice can arise that tells us: "See, this isn't the real you." By definition, this means that what the flesh wants is the real you and what it doesn't want is not the real you! Taken to its logical end, this would mean that the vast majority of men on the planet, if they were being completely authentic in pursuing their true selves, would have a lifestyle similar to Hugh Hefner's! This is where the male of the species ends up if the flesh is unrestrained. Our present *zeitgeist* or cultural ethos is awash with a promotion of self-discovery, being the real you, and following your heart. The damage to the human soul is incalculable if the real you is synonymous with the flesh.

A fourth false voice I've heard in the spiritual landscape is what I call the voice of substitution. This voice says you can jettison traditional spiritual disciplines—prayer, Bible study, meditation, attending church, engagement in the sacraments—and substitute them with "finding God in everyday life." I'm a strong advocate of finding God in everyday life—seeing his goodness in the waitress's smile, his beauty in the desert wildflower, and his truth in a well-crafted movie. In fact, finding such things through the eyes of faith is a discipline in itself. However, such a discipline is supposed to be an addition to the other disciplines and not a substitution for them. My experience tells me that those Christians who try to substitute traditional spiritual disciplines with finding God in everyday life often end up losing both.

In all this talk about embracing spiritual disciplines, it is good to remember that the mercies of God endure forever. This means that God does not despise small beginnings and understands that the young Christian may begin with only ten minutes of prayer in the morning and then gradually, over the years, build on that. It means that God understands dry seasons and is also compassionate to people who have had a recent trauma.

One couple I know were innocent bystanders in an ugly church split. They were original members of the church and actively involved in significant ministries. They told me that for months after the split, they were so devastated the only prayer they could offer up was "Jesus! Jesus! Jesus! Help me! Help me! Help me!" That isn't Shakespeare but it was good enough for a God abounding in compassion. The primary question to ask ourselves in assessing our level of spiritual engagement is this: What is the overall trend or trajectory of our relationship to spiritual disciplines over the months and years? Is there a gradual trend of growth or drawing back?

Also, please remember in your endeavor to have a vibrant spiritual life that "the just man falls seven times and rises again" (Proverbs 24:16). As Winston Churchill said to the British people during World War II, "Never, never, never, never give up." When you fall, be careful not to be too hard on yourself. Many

Christians are a lot harder on themselves than God is on them. And please remember Father Hewitt's advice not to try to bench press 300 pounds your first day of weight training.

That's all for now. I'm off to bed with an excellent spy thriller novel. The book is ending and the mastermind terrorist is about to get his comeuppance. I'm looking forward to it.

God bless you and keep you.

Under the Tender Mercies,
Uncle Aaron

CHAPTER 5

Dear Carson, Dennis, Greg, Paul, Bill, and Alan:

It's been rain, rain, rain here for five days. I definitely did pick the right time to read *The Brothers Karamazov* again—a profound and long book—and have caught up on almost all my letter writing. Before the rain came, I enjoyed a wonderful three-day weekend with a cousin of mine from the Seattle area. He's a Presbyterian and a successful corporate executive who called me, saying he "needed a break from three-piece suits, brokering deals, and trying to be the smartest guy in the room."

While drinking some very good oatmeal stout on the deck of my cabin, he said "You know, Aaron, the Church is good at seeing the potential harvest among the down-and-outers but can be blind to the harvest among the up-and-outers." From time to time, he has been an effective witness to people he says who "have attained the American Dream but are left singing the old Peggy Lee song 'Is That All There Is?' or, worse yet, with some, that dream has become a nightmare."

Fishing was slow at my favorite spots on the Columbia so we packed a picnic lunch and drove about five miles south of Fawn Creek to Cedar Creek. Cedar Creek is the ideal waterway for me. Without too much effort, you can have all the blessings of a classic north-eastern Washington stream without seeing another human being. Four- and five-foot waterfalls flow over large rocks into pools where pan-sized brook trout hide in the shadows. Some of the larger boulders have vine maples growing out of the crevices and a rock wall goes up about 150 feet. I keep expecting to see a cougar prowling about up there but I never do. Stands of cedar grow close to the creek and the smell of wet cedar is sometimes mixed with the smell of warm pine needles on a summer day. Driftwood scattered here and there high up on a rocky hillside bear silent witness to the waterway's more voluminous past.

The unmistakable "voice" of the creek says "Don't rush; slow down." I mention this to my cousin and he admits that every bad deal he's ever made in the corporate world was rushed. He now has a quote on the wall in his office by Lao Tzu that says "Nature does not hurry yet everything is accomplished." He shares this with me as we walk among the moss and lichen in the dappled sunlight.

The fishing was pretty good but we threw them all back except for a ten-incher that swallowed my hook. Some driftwood near the highest waterfall became our "park bench" as we lunched on roast beef sandwiches, lemonade, potato salad, and Snickers bars. We talked about the Mariners and the Seahawks and my cousin's golf game. He said, "The more I practice the worse I get. I can't seem to get my arms around it."

His countenance became more serious and he repeated what I've heard many middle-aged men say: "In fact, I can't seem to get my arms around anything in life. I have an MBA from a prestigious university and have no idea where this economy is going. You'd be better off asking your plumber where this economy is going than me. I can't get my arms around my marriage. What worked ten years ago isn't working anymore. There's no talk about separation or divorce but we need to make major changes and probably need a marriage counselor. I can't get my arms around my kids. My daughter leaves for the mission field next month while my son just entered rehab for drug addiction. It's interesting how I won't allow myself to take any of the credit for my daughter, but somehow I take most of the blame for my son."

It was one of those moments where I had nothing to say but felt more moved by the Spirit simply to be a supportive presence. Never underestimate the influence of a loving presence. Tradition suggests that St. Francis of Assisi told his novice to "preach the Gospel at all times and when necessary use words."

When he left, I only had four words for him: "This too shall pass." His eyes registered a deep acknowledgment, he thanked me for the weekend, and said he felt re-energized and "ready to muddle through this mystery called life."

Carson, thanks for the phone call that came shortly before my cousin arrived. I'm glad to hear exams and papers are done for almost all of you and that everyone wants to take a long break from all things academic. Your planned camping trip with Alan to Ruby Lake sounds great. I had good luck there for walleye about fifty yards off Mackey Point and caught some nice smallmouth bass near the lodge this time of year.

I'm delighted the group appreciated my last two letters and respect their honesty in sharing present frustrations. It can be discouraging to be a young Christian on the way to the Idaho silver strike—i.e., a spiritually engaged person who has had an authentic conversion—and still have significant struggles. Again, I wish there was some formula for change but there isn't. There seems to be as many ways to grow and change as there are sins and struggles to overcome.

I have seen people go through major changes at initial conversion to Christ and have seen them continue to grow as they embrace spiritual disciplines. I have even seen some progress through the formulaic approach and have concluded that God is so merciful and compassionate he will sometimes overlook this folly for a season. Some people have grown because of the fear of God: "If I keep doing this, I'm going straight to hell." Some people have changed because of the love of God: "I love Jesus too much to keep offending him by acting this way." Mature Christians usually have a healthy balance of fear and love.

Many Christians need to go through some sort of crisis before they have a breakthrough. A stubborn sin buffets them day and night. They try to fight the problem through self-effort. Eventually, the self-effort fuel runs out. They are exhausted and humbled and cry out for divine assistance. In this posture of dependence, Jesus comes and cleanses their inner leper and brings healing and deliverance. In contrast, I have seen other people go through major changes without the need of some great crisis.

Again, as I said in the previous letter, prepare yourself for some protracted struggles against sin and human weakness. Strap in for the long haul. The Roman Catholic Church teaches that in the sacrament of holy baptism, all of our sins—original sin and offenses committed by our own will—were completely cleansed. However, baptism does not deliver us from the weakness of our own nature—i.e., the gravity pull of sin within us or what theologians call *concupiscence*. Every orthodox, biblical branch or denomination in the Christian faith clearly teaches that we will battle sin until the day we die.

George Washington, our first president and by all accounts a man of sterling character, struggled with a bad temper at an age when many of us will be collecting social security. My priest, Father Hewitt, tells the story of a holy man of the desert who lived an ascetic lifestyle during the days of the early church. He had a novice under him who wanted to pursue the same vocation as the holy man. He was discouraged because he was battling sexual lust. He grew frustrated in the fight and finally asked the holy man: "At what point in our journey are we no longer battling sexual lust?" The holy man, without pausing, said, "They tell me three days *after* they put you in the ground."

I write these things so that you will not grow weary or become discouraged. A strong case can be made that the primary concern of the author of the Book of Hebrews was not so much that his audience would leave the Christian faith for Judaism, but that they were becoming *tired* because of the high call of Christ (Hebrews 6:1–12). A friend of a friend who was a former Golden Gloves boxer and now works in an urban ministry for at-risk youth told my friend, "Sometimes, I simply get tired of being good. I want to go out on the town and party. I want to break things and hurt people and leave the bar with the prettiest girl." He doesn't act on these impulses but still feels the power of them even after being a Christian for eighteen years.

There is much good that can come out of a long struggle. I admit that I feel some tension in saying this. Would it have been better for George Washington to get a handle on his temper early in life? Of course it would. At the same time, God can work redemptively in situations that are not ideal, and the benefits of a protracted battle are undeniable.

The nation of Israel had experienced many victories over their enemies under the leadership of Joshua. Another generation arose during the time of the Judges who had no experience in war. Because of this, God allowed certain enemy nations (e.g., Philistia) to remain in the land in order to teach the untested Israelites warfare (Judges 3:1-4). Even after initial conversion, baptism, and engagement in spiritual disciplines, everyone in the study group still finds that there are "enemies in the land" of their life. Welcome to a club that throughout history includes billions of people. However, the enemies you fight are not the Philistines, the Canaanites, and the Sidonians—the enemies you fight are the world, the flesh, and the devil. If God would have insulated you in a cocoon of complete grace and had not allowed you to battle the world, the flesh, and the devil, you would never learn warfare.

In this sheltered condition, you would be like many trust fund babies who, because of vast inherited wealth, never have to work a day in their lives. They never have to toil to pay the rent or make payroll. Their idea of a tough break is when room service at their favorite hotel closes at 11 p.m. Often, there is something profoundly missing in their character—they have not been battle-tested.

Presently, many of you may find yourself in a frustrating battle with some sin, but, if you patiently endure the fight, you will emerge wiser because of the warfare. My second-cousin, the chemical dependency counselor, doesn't recommend that anyone struggle with alcohol like he did, but he emerged wiser in the aftermath. He learned the wisdom of HALT (!) or, put another way, that he was more vulnerable to abusing alcohol when he was hungry, angry, lonely, and/or tired. He's convinced that demonic efforts were more effective on his soul during these times and the allure or "romance of drinking" that the world promotes felt more seductive. He has scores of insights just like these that emerged from a protracted struggle.

Macarius, the great monk who composed the Macarian Homilies in the fourth century, rightly contends that if God would have insulated us from a battle with the world, the flesh, and the devil, we would soon become conceited and fall just as Satan fell. A series of unbroken successes usually leads to a downfall rooted in pride. "The just man falls seven times and rises again" (Proverbs 24:16). The process of falling and rising again keeps one humble and grounded in reality. Again, this is *not* an invitation to sin but only recognizes how God, in his infinite mercies, can bring good out of a lengthy up-and-down struggle.

A friend of mine from seminary who became a military chaplain married a woman who came from a family where her father was not emotionally available and her mother was controlling and passive-aggressive. Out of this came a twenty-year battle with a variety of painful issues that she chronicled in an article in a popular Christian woman's magazine. Over coffee one morning with her husband and me ten years ago, she surprised me by saying, "You know, Aaron, I wouldn't want anyone to go through what I went through. Often I was envious of other women who seemed to receive healing and deliverance related to major emotional issues early in their Christian journey. They'd have these amazing testimonies of transformation at twenty-four or twenty-five years of age! But, now, as I sit here, I wouldn't trade my journey for theirs. Whether I was feeling the pain of being sinned against or acting out in a bad way because of my wounds, there was an earnest pursuit of God that emerged in the affliction. And out of that pursuit arose an intimacy with Jesus that wouldn't have developed had I experienced an early breakthrough. The pain I felt and the pain I dished out drove me to my knees in a profound way. Clinging to Jesus off and on for twenty years has its own reward."

Is loving intimacy with the Father, Son, and Holy Spirit even a possibility if we are insulated in a cocoon of complete grace and sheltered from the Great Battle with the world, the flesh, and the devil? I don't think so. In such a state, we would be spiritual automatons without free will, and, without free will, there is no love because love, by definition, must be chosen. Christ our Bridegroom wants a Bride who has chosen him over competing lovers (all created things). A protracted struggle, even with all its ups and downs, provides a suitable context for such a choice.

As you embrace this battle on the road to the Idaho silver strike, I leave you with these wise and encouraging words from C. S. Lewis:

> I know all about the despair of overcoming chronic temptations. It is not serious, provided self-offended petulance, annoyance at breaking records, impatience, etc., don't get the upper hand. No amount of falls will really undo us if we keep on picking ourselves up each time. We shall of course be very muddy and tattered children by the time we reach home, but the bathrooms are all ready, the towels put out, and the clean clothes in the airing cupboard. The only fatal thing is to lose one's temper and give it up. It is when we notice the dirt that God is most present in us: it is the very sign of his presence.
>
> *The Business of Heaven*

Under the Tender Mercies,
Uncle Aaron

CHAPTER 6

Dear Carson, Dennis, Greg, Paul, Bill, Alan, and John:

Welcome, John, as a new member of the Bible Study Group! Carson spoke highly of you in our last phone conversation. As a doctoral candidate in chemistry, it would've been helpful to have had a friend like you in high school. My GPA in high school took minor hits from both chemistry and trigonometry. I'm definitely a man of letters and not a man of science.

It appears my early summer high jinks have caught up with me. Last Friday, Grant McKittrick, a cattle rancher and member of my church, gave me a guided tour of his ranch near Henshaw Lake. I've always been smitten by the Great American West and, in this tour, overindulged in my cowboy fantasies (Me being a cowboy is tantamount to me being the top student in John's chemistry program). I simply overdid it in helping Grant with some basic chores. After a rough night of sleep, I woke up, and during a light breakfast, remembered that Rick Longstreet, the owner of the place where I live, said that a painter was coming Wednesday to the cabin to do some painting, staining, and varnishing. Since I did some painting in college and seminary, I decided to do some staining and varnishing inside in order to save Rick some money. Not a good idea.

A number of factors converged to create my present bedridden state. Overdoing it at the McKittrick ranch, a lousy night of sleep, an almost-empty stomach from a light breakfast, nausea from staining and varnishing in a poorly ventilated room, stress from working with a spatter-happy stain, and the ever-present CFS put me on my back by noon and kept me there for the next twenty-four hours.

For the last two days, I've assumed what I call "the writer's position" or "the pray the rosary position." Sitting up in bed with two pillows behind me against the wall, I can pray the rosary, write letters, or maybe watch a little TV (or a DVD) at night. I get up only for food or to go to the bathroom. In another day, I hope to get back to normal activities. For the time being, I'm sitting here in a frustrating mental fog punctuated by occasional windows of clarity when I can actually drop a line to a friend or family member. And if there's nothing good on TV, I alternate at night between *The Brothers Karamazov* and a spy thriller novel. I now theorize that perhaps Ivan Karamazov lost his sanity in the book because he had CFS and didn't know it!

Because my present perspective has a somewhat surreal quality, I reread my past letters to the Study Group and was relieved to find them coherent and relatively free of tangents and digressions. This morning, I actually had to revisit and reconfirm *why* I am writing these letters in the first place. Again, I rejoiced that I hadn't forgotten even though I feared that I had forgotten. I even wrote down a thumbnail sketch of my mission:

Help Study Group get to the Gold Rush which is code for hearing Christ say, "Well done, you good and faithful servant" at the Throne of God.

One challenge in writing these letters is that religious language, like any other kind of language, becomes exhausted, and timeless truths can lose their freshness to the audience. For example, I can write that it is important for the Christian to not only make Jesus their Savior but also to make him their Lord. This is a timeless truth whose expression has become hackneyed from overuse. Such is the challenge set before me in continuing to write this letter, and because of this challenge, I begin with a biblical theology that is anything but trite:

> *One thing* I ask of the Lord; this I seek: To dwell in the Lord's house all the days of my life, To gaze on the Lord's beauty, to visit his temple.
>
> Psalm 27:4

> The Lord said to her in reply, "Martha, Martha, you are anxious and worried about many things. There is need of only *one thing*. Mary has chosen the better part and it will not be taken from her."
>
> Luke 10:41

> Brothers, I for my part do not consider myself to have taken possession. Just *one thing:* Forgetting what lies behind but straining forward to what lies ahead, I continue my pursuit

> toward the goal, the prize of God's upward calling, in Christ Jesus.
>
> Philippians 3:13, 14

The italics in all three passages are mine and serve to underscore a common theme. Amidst the attacks of malicious enemies, David responds by seeking God's face (v. 8), dwelling in his temple, and gazing upon his beauty (v. 4). In the midst of domestic hustle and bustle, Martha succumbs to anxiety and worry while Mary has made the better choice in sitting at Christ's feet and listening to him speak (v. 39). In the midst of opposition from heretical teachers (v. 2) and a busy apostolic ministry, the apostle Paul considers everything as rubbish except for the "supreme good of knowing Christ Jesus…" (v. 8). Though they have significantly different contexts, all three passages emphasize the one supreme good of pursuing an intimate relationship with God.

Perhaps a more analytical reader in the Study Group will notice that David in Psalm 27 is pursuing intimacy with God the Father while Mary and Paul are pursuing intimacy with God the Son. What should be emphasized, though, is that the Trinity are both distinct persons but indivisible. Put another way, the Trinity cannot be cut and divided up like a chicken—breast, thigh, drumstick, wing, etc. When you pursue intimacy with one person, you'll get intimacy with the other two. Jesus said that he and the Father are one and that "whoever has seen me has seen the Father" (John 14:9).

The same careful reader in the Study Group may also notice that Paul not only is pursuing an intimate knowledge of Christ but he is also seeking to become like Christ. He wants to be like Christ in his resurrection and sufferings (v. 10), and, in his correspondence to the Romans, he emphasizes God's ultimate plan of conforming the redeemed souls to the image of his Son. Again, this is a case of, if you have one, you'll have the other—if you're pursuing intimacy with God, you are also in the process of becoming like Christ. Think of older couples that have an intimacy based on self-giving love. People often comment that, as the years go by, they start to look like each other. Or to use an illustration from a past letter about thespians: an up-and-coming young actress who idolizes Meryl Streep will often begin to resemble Streep in gestures, countenance, and speech patterns. We become like who we adore and who we are intimate with.

One more point can be added here: When the redeemed pursue an intimate relationship with Christ, they not only become like Christ but they also will make Christ known to the watching world. All three of these pursuits are inextricably bound together. Remember again what tradition says St. Francis said to his novice. He knew that Christ-likeness without a verbal expression was a witness in itself. Paul affectionately called the Corinthians his epistle written not with ink (2 Corinthians 3:2, 3).

Dear Study Group—Carson, Dennis, Greg, Paul, Bill, Alan, and John—at this juncture in my correspondence to you I can make you this promise without equivocation: If you single-mindedly pursue intimacy with the Father, Son, and Holy Spirit, the rest of your lives, you will (1) become like Christ, (2) make him known to the watching world and, (3) hear "Well done, you good and faithful servant" after you die and stand before him in heaven. Yes, you will make it to a heavenly Klondike and mine a gold rush beyond your wildest dreams because "eye has not seen, nor ear heard, nor has the human heart comprehended what God has prepared for those who love him." (1 Corinthians 2:9)

The aforementioned promise is easier said than done. I can make you another promise without equivocation: if you are proactively headed to a heavenly Klondike, get ready for a cage match to the death in this life with the world, the flesh, and the devil. If Satan cannot take you with him to hell, he will do everything he can to hinder your growth in this life.

Notice how I used the word "single-mindedly" in the first promise. Human beings are a distracted species. I have a confession: I love God but I doubt few people struggle more with a wandering mind during mass or while praying the rosary than me. Sometime in the next year or two, please read the Book of Judges. It is like the human heart writ large with the nation of Israel displaying in the macro what is a reality in the micro. The nation of Israel, a corporate entity, reveals what often goes on in the individual human heart. The narrative is a perpetual cycle of distraction, decline, and idolatry followed by spiritual and national renewal under God's chosen leaders (Deborah, Gideon, Samson, et al).

The formidable thinker Dennis Prager on his radio show says, "The human being is not an impressive species." Father Hewitt contends that about 10 percent of the world are made up of saints and near saints. Another 10 percent, he says, are comprised of the evil and the near evil. The remaining 80 percent, he speculates, are a mixed bag. He calls the church he pastors (St. Matthew's) "Church of the Mixed Bag." I don't write these things to discourage the Study Group—I write these things in the hopes of driving each person to their knees with Jesus' words on their lips "…without me you can do nothing" (John 15:15).

Years ago, as a young pastor, after many distractions that were often rooted in narcissism, I committed my life, like David, Mary, and Paul, to The Pursuit of the One Thing. My mentor and spiritual director at the time was the late, great Conrad Kersten. Conrad was such a spiritual giant that adjectives used at his funeral such as "profound, wise, loving, sacrificial," etc., actually felt redundant, like saying "wet water."

One day, over a cup of coffee at his favorite diner, he told me, "You know, Aaron, it's good that you're pursing intimacy with God but I think you may have overlooked one important thing: The Father, Son, and Holy Spirit are also pursuing you but with infinitely more resolve and incomprehensible love." Conrad was right. I had overlooked this, or at least his pithy summary greatly helped me make the journey from mere mental assent to a doctrine (God loves me) to an epiphany that continues to nourish my soul.

Early on in our marriage, both my late wife Claire and I, for very different reasons, struggled with the concept of God's incomprehensible love and passionate pursuit of intimacy with us. Claire's father was an alcoholic who left his wife and three kids when Claire was ten years old. Though she eventually forgave her dad and reconciled with him, for many years her concept of God the Father was inextricably linked to who her earthly father was—not there for her in any important way. Conrad's wisdom served as a catalyst that began a journey of healing damaged emotions and introducing her to a loving, heavenly Father.

My struggles came from a different place. Many encouraging things happened to me during the first decade of my pastorate, but it was also a crash course in a class called Flawed Humanity 101. Individuals and entire families left the church for petty reasons. My youth pastor had to resign because of sexual immorality and an elder-in-training never became an elder because he was caught embezzling funds from both his job and our church. Underhanded power plays were made by members of the "old guard" on different church committees because the church was moving in a new direction that threatened their influence. I received complaints on a variety of issues: The sermon was too long; the sermon was too short. Worship and singing were too long; worship and singing were too short. Too many hymns; not enough hymns. The music was too contemporary; the music was too traditional. Adult Education should be before the main service; Adult Education should be after the main service. Nothing in the church building should be changed; bulldoze the building and start over. I could go on and on but you get the point.

Despite the presence of many wonderful parishioners, the experience of seeing certain people's warts and all and the growing revelation of my own warts compelled me to question the wisdom of God: "God, human beings are an unimpressive species. We are a grubby lot—proud, vain, and ungrateful. Why make such an effort with us? Why sacrifice your only Son to redeem us and pursue an intimate relationship with us? Wouldn't it have been easier and better to invest in beings that are less flawed and just a bit more angelic? We don't deserve your tender mercies." I was right. We don't deserve his tender mercies but that's the nature of his mercy and grace—it's undeserved favor. I have much more to say on the subjects broached in this letter but I need to go lie down for awhile. I'll pick up where I left off. Until then, I am…

Under the Tender Mercies,
Uncle Aaron

CHAPTER 7

Dear Carson, Dennis, Greg, Paul, Bill, Alan, and John:

After some time on my back, I began to feel better and spent the good part of yesterday running errands. Now I'm back to the "writer's position." When I ended my last letter, I was exploring my confusion at God's love and passionate pursuit of us in the light of our human frailty. Again, God's tender mercies don't make sense to us because they're not based on human merit. Put another way, God's grace would make sense to us if it was deserved, but it would no longer be amazing grace. At some point, we just have to admit that this is where human understanding gives way to a Great Mystery.

When my son Jeremy was a baby, I had an old bathrobe that had been through the "baby wars." Let's just say that that bathrobe became the indiscriminate target of every bodily function that boy had—sometimes all in one day! And yet, at the end of the day, the bathrobe would go into the wash, Jeremy would be put down in his crib, and my fatherly love for him was undiminished. The experience of being a father spoke more to me about the incomprehensible love of God than all the volumes of theology I've read over the years.

You may balk at the idea of God passionately pursuing an intimate relationship with you for whatever reason just as Claire and I did. My advice is to ground yourself in the biblical narrative and it will increase your faith because faith comes from hearing the word of God (Romans 10:17). From Genesis to Revelation, there is a uniform testimony of (1) humanity falling from grace into sin, (2) God providing a means of redeeming people, and (3) one of the major purposes of redemption being the intimate communion of God and his people.

The events of the Book of Exodus are breathtaking. Moses is groomed as the deliverer for Israel. God sends ten plagues upon the nation of Egypt until Pharaoh finally lets the chosen people of Israel go. Pharaoh changes his mind and sends men on chariots to bring the Israelites back. God parts the Red Sea and brings Israel to safety while moments later the same sea collapses on the Egyptians. Then begins a narrative of God's supernatural provision for his people: manna from heaven, a cloud blocking the sun by day, and a pillar of fire to light their way at night just to name some of the miracles. God went to great lengths to redeem Israel and one of his major motivations was to have a people who would be a "kingdom of priests, a holy nation" (Exodus 19:6), offering sacrifices to him in a close relationship.

This ground has been plowed over and over. We all know that the pinnacle of God's efforts came in the Incarnation. God *so loved* the world he gave his only begotten Son (John 3:16). He did not spare his own

Son and wishes to freely give us all things (Romans 8:32). The Father has bestowed great love on us in calling us the children of God (1 John 3:1). Could there be any greater love than a crucified God who endured an unspeakably heinous death in order to redeem his creation for relationship?

When God the Father saw that Adam was alone, he made Eve a partner suitable for him, because it was not good for man to be alone. When God the Father looked at his Son (the second Adam), he also saw that he was alone and began, in his eternal counsels, to prepare a bride for him. Like Eve, this bride would be bone of his bone and flesh of his flesh, and the two of them will become one body (Genesis 2:23, 24). This bride will be a Church that Christ has died for, sanctified, cleansed, and will present to himself in all its splendor without spot or wrinkle, holy and without blemish (Ephesians 5:21–33). The actual wedding of Christ and his bride will take place in heaven when it will be announced, "Let us rejoice and be glad and give him glory. For the wedding day of the Lamb has come, his bride has made herself ready" (Revelation 19:7).

Any discussion of God's great love and desire for intimacy with us would be incomplete without looking at the great discourse on the Bread of Life (John 6:22–59) that culminated in Jesus' hard saying in Capernaum:

> ...Amen, amen, I say to you, unless you eat the flesh of the Son of Man and drink his blood, you do not have life within you. Whoever eats my flesh and drinks my blood has eternal life, and I will raise him on the last day. For my

> flesh is true food and my blood is true drink. Whoever eats my flesh and drinks my blood remains in me and I in him.
>
> John 6:53–56

In writing this letter to seven people, I understand that there will be different views on holy communion, from it being a sacrament that is symbolic of our unity with Christ to it being the real presence—the actual body and blood, soul and divinity of the Lord Jesus Christ. What is clear, however, is that whatever view you embrace on this sacrament, Christ himself was pursuing a degree of intimacy with his followers, i.e., his bride, heretofore unimagined and unsurpassed in the history of the biblical narrative.

My mentor Conrad Kersten also said, "We are supposed to be involved in a divine romance, but if we are unaware and not experiencing Christ's passionate pursuit of us, then it's nothing more than unrequited love."

Claire and I met our freshman year in college and were friends for a year before the romantic dimension of our relationship blossomed. A friend of mine asked why I didn't ask her out on a date. I told him I was getting over a broken heart from a relationship in high school and, "Besides, Claire is too good-looking and out of my league." What I found out later was that, although she did date another guy off and on her freshman year, she was interested in me and hoped I would ask her out. She later told me, "I dropped some subtle hints but you were dumb as a box of rocks."

When I finally did ask her out and she said yes, a light bulb went on in my head and my heart and I began to see the past subtle hints for what they really were. The romantic overtures I extended to her were returned in kind. I was pursuing her and she was pursuing me and that in turn *energized* my pursuit of her. You may have already committed yourself to the pursuit of the one thing, but to be acutely aware of the Trinity's passionate pursuit of you will give you a double portion of encouragement for your divine romance.

This new awareness may result in some new imagery that you may begin to see with the eyes of your heart (Ephesians 1:18): the loving eyes of the bridegroom, the warm embrace of the Father of Lights, and the close companionship of the Holy Spirit. For Catholics and Orthodox believers, one or more icons may take on a wonderful new significance.

It isn't that the love-drunk God has cast his affectionate eyes on you for the first time. No, like Claire and my relationship in college, the Eyes of Love have been upon you all along. Christ said, "It was not you who chose me, but I who chose you and appointed you to go and bear fruit that will remain…" (John 15:16). The apostle John who recorded this saying in his Gospel also wrote, "We love because He first loved us" (1 John 4:19). He made the first move; he wanted us.

Few things are more seductive than the awareness of being wanted. Carlos Olivas, who has a fruitful ministry in planting churches in the Mexican-American community, once spoke at my seminary and told the graduating class, "Be careful when you're interviewing for your first church job after you graduate. A church may really want you but it could very well be the last church on earth you want to serve. Never underestimate the seductive power of being wanted. Make your decision with much prayer and at least two or three advisors."

Several years ago, as a pastor, I had the unenviable task of sorting through the wreckage of a troubled marriage in my church. The wife's behavior fit a familiar pattern. Growing up, she felt unwanted by her neglectful father and went out and married a man just like her father. She later realized that she married her husband in order to fix things with her dad: "I guess I was trying to get it right the second time around."

As a legal secretary, she eventually had a five-year affair with a lawyer at the firm where they met. She said, "I held off his advances for awhile but he eventually wore me down. He wasn't especially handsome or successful but he really wanted me and that made me feel alive. Several times, out of tremendous guilt, I wanted to end it but I couldn't do it because I loved being wanted."

Shortly after these confessions, I referred the couple to an excellent marriage counselor in town. The wife gave up her affair, got a new job, and wholeheartedly returned to the evangelical faith of her youth. The husband attended a few counseling sessions but continued his pattern of neglect. The marriage ended six months later when he left her for a younger woman he met at work.

In recent years, there's been an abundance of movies, television shows, and literature inhabited by central characters who are vampires. A common pattern I've noticed in these offerings is the narrative of a male vampire who wants a female human (non-vampire) with more intensity than your average male-female (non-vampire) romantic relationship. This extreme passion seems to resonate with a younger female audience who want to be wanted in the extreme.

In human relationships, because of the seductive power of being wanted, it is wise to proceed with both caution and prudence and, in the case of the woman who had the five-year affair, to not proceed at all! With God the Father, God the Son, and God the Spirit, my advice, however, is to drop your guard and let yourself be seduced! Let the biblical narrative be a love letter that you respond to in kind. Conrad Kersten, before he died, told me, "If I was to write an autobiography, I'd call it *The Seduction of a Good Man*. My wife always told me 'You're a good man, Conrad.' God chose me first; He wanted me. My life has simply been a response to that, a seduction of sorts."

With a study group composed exclusively of young men, I anticipate a question I received from a young man in my church years ago: "It doesn't seem fair. Christian women can very easily slide into the bride-bridegroom relationship with Christ because they are women and he is the Eternal Man. They then get to enjoy all the benefits of this spiritual romance. I love Jesus but I'm a guy and feel uncomfortable assuming the female role. What am I to do?"

When such questions are raised, I identify with David in Psalm 139:6: "Such knowledge is beyond me, far too lofty for me to reach," or Psalm 131:1: "I do not busy myself with great matters, with things too sublime for me." We are brushing shoulders with a Great Mystery; we are shaking hands with a Reality who is brimming with paradox. I proceed with caution but I think what I do have to say almost every orthodox Christian will agree with.

For one, it is easier for Christian women to assume the role of betrothed or bride to Christ's bridegroom. However, these same women can say it feels unfair to them that the vast majority of images for God in the Bible are undeniably masculine and that God—Father, Son, and Holy Spirit—is called "he" by orthodox believers. The apostle Paul says that our knowledge is limited in this life and that "we see through a glass darkly" (1 Corinthians 13:12). On this side of eternity, we will struggle with male and female imagery related to God; on the other side, these mysteries will be understood.

The Wholly Other God is radically distinct from the created order and that includes male and female:

> In no way is God in man's image. He is neither man nor woman. God is pure spirit in which there is no place for the difference between the sexes. But the respective "perfections" of man and woman reflect something of the infinite perfection of God: those of a mother and those of a father and husband.
>
> Catechism of the Catholic Church #370

Statements such as these render much of acrimony over inclusive language moot. In the light of the reality of the Wholly Other God, it is wise not to anthropomorphize God too much either way, male or female.

Don't create God in our image. There is an infinite qualitative difference between who God is and who we are.

However, in answering the question of the young man in my church years ago—"What am I to do?"—there is an undeniable feminine imagery related to God. There has been a debate in recent years about the Holy Spirit because there is an unmistakable feminine imagery—both maternal and bridal—ascribed to the Spirit in Old Testament sources, the early Church fathers, and the writings of outstanding orthodox modern theologians who have explored these themes.

Suppose someone from the Study Group wrote me and said, "Today, as I walked through the woods and was communing with the Holy Spirit, I experienced feminine imagery. I felt cherished and wanted. I felt like I was on a date." I'd say, "Great," but I'd also encourage this person to not cling to these images too dogmatically because many of our conceptions of God will either evaporate or be extensively revised when we see him as he is (1 John 3:2) in the effable light of his boundless goodness, beauty, and truth.

Under the Tender Mercies,
Uncle Aaron

CHAPTER 8

Dear Carson, Dennis, Greg, Paul, Bill, Alan, and John:

Greetings from beautiful northeast Washington! The painter had a death in the family and showed up a week later than expected along with another tradesman who came to replace the linoleum. The linoleum was poorly installed and is curling up here and there with a color that was undoubtedly popular when Mary Tyler Moore had a hit television show. Because of the fumes from the stain and varnish and the floor guy needing to work in the kitchen, bathroom, and hallway outside the bathroom, I decided to spend a few days in Clayton with my friends Don and Kathryn Yarbrough.

Clayton, as you may remember, is the nearest town of any size to Fawn Creek (population 7,500) and is where I attend mass and do most of my shopping, grocery, and otherwise. The Yarbroughs attend St. Matthew's and are retired after owning a successful chain of restaurants in the Seattle–Tacoma area. When I'm with Don, I always know I'll be hoisting excellent Sumatra coffee in the morning and equally as enjoyable red wine for dinner at night. Kathryn is not a coffee drinker but knows more about wine than anyone I know. She also made some comments about Clayton that resonated with my own impressions:

"I grew up in a small town in Kansas," she said, "about the same size as Clayton and similar in personality and values." In both towns, she said, "Hard work and Judeo-Christian values were assumed whether you attended church or not. It wasn't 100 percent like a Norman Rockwell painting, don't get me wrong. There were patches of a seedy underbelly here and there and like every other town had every imaginable human weakness on display. For example, my dentist left his wife and three kids for the dental hygienist!"

The rest of what I write here is a combination of additional comments Kathryn made with my own thoughts. Many Claytonians, if they don't embrace Christ as Lord and Savior, are what Flannery O'Connor described as "haunted by Christ." They were raised Christian but, going against their upbringing, sit in the local tavern ogling the provocatively dressed young woman at the next table. Like Augustine, before his conversion, they tell themselves that "Chastity may be a good idea but not tonight."

Many who are not confessing Christians are, nonetheless, haunted by a Christian upbringing. Many who don't *explicitly* embrace the Judeo-Christian value system do so *implicitly*. Because of this, I think there is a greater per capita collective wisdom in Clayton than many of our elite universities that are lauded as "enlightened" and "sophisticated." Here I pilfer and revise the famous quote from the late William F. Buckley in saying that I'd rather randomly take 200 names from the

Clayton phone book and have them run the country than 200 professors from either Yale or Harvard.

Much has been written about the importance of knowing the incomprehensible love of God for us in my last two letters and by other authors in the last three decades. Years ago, I had an experience that served to sharpen my understanding about this emphasis. As the church I pastored grew, we began to draw a small but influential contingent of writers, artists, and intellectuals into the congregation. For me, this equated with "influencing the culture" and I was delighted one Sunday after church service when a novelist of note and a professor of psychology (both women) wanted to share with me their "vision of expanding the kingdom of God." I went to bed that night excited about the gospel of Christ making in-roads into academia and among the literati. Unfortunately, after I had lunch with them the next day, I never saw either of them again.

Their vision of expanding the kingdom of God actually came down to them wanting to reform the church I pastored so that we would attract new members. Amiable and sincere, they both opened our discussion with a hope of dialogue and civility that reminded me of something I had heard on National Public Radio years before. The novelist then launched out into more controversial waters: "Both of us think and feel that there is nothing more important than knowing the love of God. We think that most problems in the Church could be solved if people met in 'encouragement groups' of four to five people once a week and simply reflected the love of God to one another in a safe, nurturing, and affirming atmosphere."

The psychology professor politely added, "The groups should avoid oughts, shoulds, and demanding calls to discipleship and should instead focus on who we are in Christ unconditionally and how much God loves us. Also," she continued, "we think you're an excellent preacher and teacher but wonder if the content of your sermons would be more emotionally healthy if it was wisely pruned of oughts, shoulds, and calls to discipleship." The conversation from both of them continued in this vein and repeatedly encouraged me to create an atmosphere that was "safe, nurturing, affirming, not shaming, and emotionally healthy." The novelist opined that perhaps this emphasis on knowing God's love should permeate every program in the church.

"For far too long," the professor said, "an unhealthy patriarchy has reigned in the Church and with the loss of the Sacred Feminine, we have lost the God who nurtures her people. We are left with an angry male sky-god who burdens his children with commandment after commandment."

Congruent with this sentiment, the novelist said, "If I could wave a magic wand, I'd make all the churches in the world have a moratorium on the so-called hot-button issues like abortion and homosexuality. Jesus didn't say anything about either issue yet many churches can't stop talking about them."

Our lunch ended amicably but with major disagreements. The thoughts I share now with the Study Group I also shared with the two women and am convinced they will help you on your journey to the northern California gold rush.

My first admonition to you is to be careful not to make any particular emphasis (e.g., knowing the love of God, prayer, evangelism, servanthood, etc.) the be-all and end-all, the panacea for every malady in your life or in your local church. Many truths are transformative like knowing the love of God but there's only one be-all and end-all and that's Jesus Christ himself. I approached the aforementioned women with humility that day because I had made a similar mistake as a young pastor.

Thank God for congregations who are patient with young clergymen. In the early years, I had a familiar pattern of encountering a particular truth, (e.g., spiritual warfare), studying it, praying and meditating about it, becoming very excited about it, and then making it the remedy for everything. After about a year of this, an elder in my parish who became like a father to me (a retired Army colonel for whom I had immense respect) joked, "Hey, Aaron, what's going to save the world this month, ministry to the poor or healing damaged emotions?"

We had a good laugh and both agreed that it's easy to become more enamored over a truth about Christ than *the* Truth, Christ himself.

"Healthy Christians are balanced Christians. Healthy churches are balanced churches," Father Hewitt recently said. To reference a shopworn comparison, eating just one food group (e.g., proteins) makes for an imbalanced diet just as embracing a particular emphasis as the alpha and omega makes for an unhealthy spiritual diet.

Think of all the different truths and emphases in the Christian life as being like all the different instruments in a philharmonic orchestra. An orchestra that has only violins would be symphonically-challenged. Some musicians in the orchestra are more important than others. For example, the sublime Vladimir Horowitz on piano is a more important musician than a fifth-chair oboe. Similarly, truths such as servanthood—the whole-hearted embrace of self-giving lifestyle—are more important than, say, an increased knowledge of the history of Israel one might gain through recent archaeological discoveries. The first emphasis when translated into the shoe-leather of life is transformative; the second, though helpful, is not.

Think of the Holy Spirit as the conductor of the philharmonic orchestra. His role is to take all the different truths and emphases and blend them into a coherent and transcendent symphony. Christ said that the Holy Spirit "will glorify me, because he will take from what is mine and declare it to you" (John 16:14). My advice to the Study Group is this: Don't let any truth or emphasis, whether of small, medium, or large importance, become an end in itself. Instead, ask the Holy Spirit to take all the different emphases you possess and blend them into a harmonious sound that magnifies Christ. Ask and it will be given to you.

When the professor and the novelist suggested that "the content of my sermons would be more emotionally healthy if it was wisely pruned of oughts, shoulds, and calls to discipleship," I thought to myself, "These women don't want a senior pastor; they want a senior therapist." When such issues arise, I often consult what some call the Christological Key, i.e., I look at the controversy through the lens of Christ's words and deeds.

As C. S. Lewis rightly pointed out in *Mere Christianity*, Christ preached more about hell than heaven. There is the Jesus who showed mercy to the woman caught in adultery (though he also exhorted her to sin no more), blessed the little children, and wanted to gather Jerusalem unto himself as a mother hen gathers her chicks under her wings. But there's also the Jesus who continually called his listeners to repentance and this "changing of mind" was always linked to oughts, shoulds, and demanding calls to discipleship.

As far as the professor's comments on abortion and homosexuality, it's probably best to explore those at a later time. However, I do embrace the traditional Catholic view on those issues and obviously don't think there should be a moratorium on talking about them.

One area of agreement that I had with the professor and the novelist was this: Knowing the love of God is often a transformative truth and stands as a Vladimir Horowitz or a Jascha Heifetz in the orchestra of emphasis. I have more to say here but am now off to a men's gin rummy game with beer and cigars with Don Yarbrough and friends. We're driving to a town near the Columbia River named Farris Falls. Grace and peace to you all.

Under the Tender Mercies,
Uncle Aaron

CHAPTER 9

Dear Carson, Dennis, Greg, Paul, Bill, Alan, and John:

Stupid, thy name is Aaron. Don't you think that a guy who recently had to lie down for an extended period of time because he was exposed to fumes from stain and varnish in a poorly ventilated room would maybe, just maybe, have significant nausea in a room with four other men, offering up billowing clouds of smoke to the cigar gods? Lucky, thy name is Aaron. Fortunately, the card game took place on a large screen porch and, secondly, a gentle breeze came through that porch in the early evening just when I was starting to turn a little green. Some ginger ale settled my stomach and my spirits were buoyed by several winning hands.

Over the years, I must admit to feeling some ambivalence concerning the emphasis called the importance of knowing the love of God. The lunch with the two women made me wary about exalting any emphasis about Christ more than Christ himself. Secondly, so much has been written by other authors in the last three decades that those forty acres seem like they've already been plowed and anything I would say would sound trite. Then there's the false assumption by many in the kingdom of God that knowing the love of God is *always* transformative. It isn't. I've known more than a few believers who know God loves them and yet live like the prodigal son.

When Jeremy was in elementary school, the public school system in our state spent millions of dollars on promoting self-esteem in the student's lives. "Greater self-esteem will raise test scores and make better human beings," one district superintendent promised. Now the evidence is in: all those millions didn't raise test scores. We now know that many of our young men in prison have high self-esteem. Some of the finest people I've ever known have marginal or below-average self-concepts. The net effect of all this causes me to take a closer look at the idea, "Just get people to feel good about themselves, either through enhancing self-esteem, or knowing the love of God, and good things will happen." And yet, and yet…when the heart of the Christian is right, the truth can be transformative:

> And I pray that you being rooted and established in love, may have power, together with all the saints, to grasp how wide and long and high and deep is the love of Christ, and to know this love that surpasses knowledge – that you may be filled to the measure of all the fullness of God.
>
> Ephesians 3:17b–19

Here the knowledge of the incomprehensible love of God is inextricably bound to being filled with the fullness of God. Can there by anything more transformative? Equally as breathtaking is what David contends in Psalms 63:4: "For your love is better than life; my lips offer you worship!" Experiencing the love of God is the only thing in the Old Testament that is regarded as superior to life itself. Again, in the orchestra of emphasis, it stands out like a Horowitz or a Heifetz.

In revisiting another analogy, imagine yourself on a trip from New York City to the Comstock Lode ("Well done, you good and faithful servant") in Virginia City, Nevada, in 1859. The Lode was the first major discovery of silver ore in the US. Think of the covered wagon you use to make the trip as your experiential knowledge of the unfathomable love of God. It shelters you from inclement weather—rain, sleet, snow, hail, etc. For the purpose of defense and mutual assistance, you band together with other people and form "wagon trains" as you trek across the Great Plains. And, even on some occasions, you may have to create a protected perimeter and "circle the wagons" when attacked by bandits or hostile Indians.

Most therapists, psychologists, and psychiatrists would agree with counselor Jeff van Vonderen, in his book *Families Where Grace is in Place*,that human beings have at least three needs beyond basic physical sustenance: they need to feel loved, accepted, and not alone (belongingness). God's perfect will and good pleasure is to provide families, friends, and a relationship with him where these fundamental needs are met. In relation to God's love for us, the apostle Paul writes that nothing can separate us from it—neither death, nor life, nor angels, nor principalities, nor present things, nor future things, nor powers, nor height, nor depth, nor any creation (Romans 8:38, 39).

What's implied in this passage from Romans is that although nothing can separate you from the love of God, several things or entities will try to alienate you from it. The world, the flesh, and the devil, i.e., all that is against God and his ways within us (the flesh) and outside of us (the world and the devil), will work together in a toxic symphony to separate you from the awareness of divine favor. Put another way, it's not a question of *if* your covered wagon will be attacked by bad weather, bandits, and hostile Indians; it's a question of *when*. In fact, with many covered wagons, it is a relentless attack.

Years ago, a twenty-seven-year-old woman sat in my office and described the relentless attack she had endured for most of her life. Her father told her she was fat, ugly, stupid, and wouldn't amount to anything. Mean kids in elementary school echoed those sentiments. An uncle molested her. Her first husband verbally abused her like her father and was a serial adulterer. She went through a divorce and became suicidal. A friend from work invited her to our church. She told me, "The love I felt at the church literally saved my life." She cried, then I cried, and then she cried again. It made everything I had gone through, everything the church had gone through, worth it.

Since there is vast literature on this subject, I freely admit that some authors are more gifted than I in communicating some of the more salient truths. But, as Peter said, "Such as I have I give unto thee" (Acts 3:6). Here are some things that have helped me over the years:

Sometimes, it's important on our way to the Comstock Lode to take a step or two back and reevaluate a situation. Often, when young, earnest Christians are struggling to walk in a new truth (or, more accurately, to embrace *the* Truth Jesus Christ in a new way), the first impulse is to re-double their efforts and try harder.

If you are struggling with experiencing the love of God, my advice is to pray the same prayer of the father of the demon-possessed boy in Mark 9:24: "…help my unbelief." Say the prayer and rest. Recently, I read about Catherine of Siena and my own love of God felt dwarfed by hers. She made me feel like I was on God's "second team." Instead of ratcheting up the self-effort, I simply asked God to "expand my capacity to love you and make me more like Catherine."

As I said in the last letter, let the biblical text become God's written declaration of love to you. Just as Christ fought the devil with the written Word of God (Matthew 4:1-11), so are we. Years ago, because I recognized that one of the primary agendas of the world, the flesh, and the devil was to annihilate the truth that we are loved, accepted, and not alone in Christ, I declared to myself and my church that Ephesians 1:3–14 would be our Declaration of Independence from these false messages.

This passage is nothing less than a portrait of a love-intoxicated God lavishing the riches of his grace on his highly-favored children. This passage is about you. *Read it. Own it. Let it in.* The various adjectives and descriptive words are a part of your spiritual birth certificate and articulate your identity in Christ:

> Blessed be the God and Father of our Lord Jesus Christ, who has blessed us in Christ with every spiritual blessing in the heavens, as he chose us in him, before the foundation of the world, to be holy and without blemish before him. In love he destined us for adoption to himself through Jesus Christ, in accord with the favor of his will, for the praise of the glory of his grace that he granted us in the beloved.
>
> In him we have redemption by his blood, the forgiveness of transgressions, in accord with the riches of his grace that he lavished upon us. In all wisdom and insight he has made known to us the mystery of his will in accord with his favor that he set forth in him as a plan for the fullness of times, to sum up all things in Christ, in heaven and on earth.
>
> In him we were also chosen, destined in accord with the purpose of the One who accomplishes all things according to the intention of his will, so that we might exist for the praise of his glory, we who first hoped in Christ. In him you also, who have heard the word of truth, the gospel of your salvation, and have believed in him, were sealed with the promised Holy Spirit, which is the first installment of our inheritance toward redemption as God's possession, to the praise of his glory
>
> Ephesians 1:3–14

If you don't understand everything in this passage, don't feel too badly because I don't either. I do know that it means that you are loved, accepted, and not alone more than you will ever know. I do know that that this identity is not based on your flawless religious performance but is based on what Christ did on the cross for you. The exhortations to live a holy life that flavor chapters four to six of Ephesians are not given so that you will earn this identity; they are given to challenge you to live consistently with the identity *you already have* as a favored child of God. Paul urges the Ephesians "to live in a manner worthy of the call you have received" (4:1).

In a Study Group of seven young men, I can imagine there is at least one person, for whatever reason, struggling with what I've said in this letter. I think we all can learn something from the woman who testified that "the love I felt at the church literally saved my life." Before she left my office, she added, "I always struggled with the idea of God loving me, but it made sense that he loved me *at least* as much as the people at church. After all, he's God and they're only people." Here, a finite reference point (people) can provide clues about the nature of an infinite reference point (God).

Almost everyone has someone in their lives—a parent, a grandparent, a sibling—who loved them in a pure and an enduring manner. Don't you think God loves you at least as much as they do? Start there and then try to imagine him loving you twice as much as they do (if you can) and you're not even coming close to the truth.

In the pursuit of an intimate knowledge of God's love, other people are indispensable. Remember that the covered wagons often formed wagon trains and, when under attack, circled the wagons for protection. Some Christians have the attitude, "God alone is sufficient; I don't need people." There are some monastic vocations where this may be true, but for 99.9 percent of the rest of the human race, it's not true. As Dennis Prager asks on his radio show, "If God alone is enough, then why did God create Eve for Adam and say that it was not good for Adam to be alone?"

Think of the experience of traveling in wagon trains as being symbolic of those relationships you need in daily life that reflect the favor of God and communicate the truth that you are loved, accepted, and not alone. Think of the experience of "circling the wagons" as being symbolic of special, excruciating trials, when the attack of the world, the flesh, and the devil is especially fierce, and you need people to be there for you in a special way. Remember, it is the antelope that strays from the herd who is especially vulnerable to predators, and, as the author of Ecclesiastes writes, "Where a lone man may be overcome, two together can resist. A three-ply cord is not easily broken."

I would be remiss if I did not mention a common error people make in the opposite direction. When support groups began to multiply in our church, it was, by and large, a grace-filled experience for the people who participated in them—the divorced, the grieving, the addicted, etc. But it became obvious in time that some people became so enamored of their group that this group became their Primary Support Group and God became their Secondary Support Group. God is supposed to be our Source, people are resources. With some people these roles got reversed. This created tension in these support groups because people make lousy gods. You can always tell when this role-reversal has taken place because a grateful spirit will be replaced by a demanding spirit. Again, people make lousy gods.

I'm back at the cabin. The linoleum and the staining and varnishing look great. The painter has another day of exterior staining tomorrow. A heat wave is supposed to come to eastern Washington. The cabin has no air conditioning so I'll need to get fans going here and there.

Adios amigos
Under the Tender Mercies,
Uncle Aaron

Dear Carson, Dennis, Greg, Paul, Bill, Alan, and John:

The day after I mailed the last letter to the Study Group, when I was thinking about the 27 year—old woman who sat in my office and the relentless rejection she had suffered, I decided to send you this brief article by Sharon Houk. It dovetails nicely with my letter and serves as a salutary supplement. Sharon is a friend I met in seminary and she now serves as an Adult Education Coordinator at an evangelical church in Fort Worth, Texas. The piece she wrote is titled "Healing the Wound of Rejection: A Helpful Beginning" and it appeared in

Healing and Recovery magazine about seven years ago. Here's the article in its entirety:

"When a child is born into the world, often the first face they see is a doctor or nurse followed by their mother and father. Then, in their early years and all the years before they leave home, they will see their parents' faces probably more than anyone else. Single—parent homes will add a different dynamic to this experience.

Over the years their parents' faces will communicate different emotions to them. In an emotionally healthy family, lots of love, acceptance, respect, and appreciation will be communicated. In an unhealthy family, just the opposite, or a confusing mixture of true and false messages, will be communicated and will leave the child with the wound of rejection.

The wound of rejection has to be one of the most difficult wounds to heal. It happens not only in parent—child relationships but in every other imaginable relationship in the human species. It cuts deep because it communicates to the person not that they are doing something wrong, but that *something is wrong with them.*

The face that they see in their mind, whether it be a parent, spouse, or employer, tells them that they are defective, second—rate, not good enough, and unlovable. For some, this face and its false messages will plague them the rest of their lives.

It would be foolish for me to pretend to try to solve a complex problem like rejection in such a brief article. However, it is not foolish for someone like me, who has felt the sting of rejection, to try to provide a helpful beginning. As someone who grew up with a verbally abusive, alcoholic father, I simply will try to pass on some of the lessons learned that have helped me.

For starters, one thing that helped me was to realize that the person who rejected me didn't reject me because I was inherently unlovable; they rejected me because they didn't have the wherewithal, inner resources, or ability to love me like I needed to be loved. *It wasn't about me; it was about them.* Embracing this truth, for many people, is the beginning of healing.

Another thing that really helped me was spending long periods of time in meditative prayer, where I see the loving and kind face of Jesus and he sees me. Catholics call this contemplative prayer. Saint Teresa of Avila said, "Contemplative prayer, in my opinion, is nothing else than a close sharing between friends."

Sometimes I will read and meditate on a story from the Gospels and put myself in the story in such a way as to receive his grace and peace. I see Jesus and he sees me and there is an intimate exchange. I am his child sitting on his lap because "such is the kingdom of God." I am the prodigal returning home to the father who runs to greet me and still loves me despite all my character flaws. He gives me the love I did not receive from my own father.

This type of meditative prayer is therapeutic for the person who has been wounded by rejection because they replace the face of the person who has wounded them and their false messages with the face of Christ and his true messages. A central question for us as we explore this issue is "Whose face are we looking at?"

Dear reader, I hope it's the face I see in the Book of Zephaniah. Please remember that what is said in this passage to Israel is even *more* true to us today who live under a better covenant:

> On that day they will say to Jerusalem, 'Do not fear, O Zion; do not let your hands hang limp. The Lord your God is with you, he is mighty to save. He will take great delight in you, he will quiet you in his love, he will rejoice over you with singing.'
>
> Zephaniah 3:16, 17

God is singing. Why? Because he is rejoicing over and delighting in us with an over—flowing, super—abundant love. This is the face of Christ that should replace the other faces that we constantly see that have given us the wound of rejection.

Additional to this, it's also important to have friends and family that become the face of Christ to us. They incarnate that delight that he has for us and we can see it in their eyes. With all these things in place, we can truly shout from the rooftops, "Let the healing begin!"

CHAPTER 10

Dear Carson, Dennis, Greg, Paul, Bill, Alan, and John:

Welcome to the blast furnace. Temperatures are in the nineties all across eastern Washington. Even Fawn Creek, close to the Canadian border and the usual gathering place of all inclement winter weather, may hit 100 degrees tomorrow.

Inside the cabin, it helps to keep the drapes closed and have a fan or two running. Fawn Creek itself—its rushing, spring-fed waters that flow over moss-covered boulders and logs coming down from Wheeler Mountain—serves as an oasis in the desert. It feels at least fifteen degrees cooler by the creek. If I didn't know better, I'd say the creek was glacier-fed, but this isn't Alaska, and there's no glacier up on Wheeler Mountain.

Yesterday, I dunked myself in a three-foot deep pool about 100 feet from the cabin in the blazing early afternoon heat. I had several "witnesses" at my "baptism." My dog Lucy, a one-year-old Border Collie, whom a friend gave me a few weeks ago, watched with priestly reverence. This dog would charge into the gates of hell to retrieve the lime-green tennis balls I throw around with great frequency. While Lucy genuflected, a great blue heron lunched on small trout fifty yards downstream, using its long legs to wade into the creek and its long, sharp bill to spear unsuspecting fish. Occasionally, I will see a kingfisher swoop down from an exposed porch, snatch a small trout, then return to that perch with the captured prey.

The flora and fauna near my "baptism" also stood at attention and respected the sacramental moment. Wild raspberries, ferns, cow parsnip, and lichen were present with silent solemnity. The stinging nettles were not given their name for nothing. Try to forget them during summer wearing shorts and a short-sleeve shirt along the creek and they will remind you of their existence with a vengeance.

Not far from my dunking pool three fifty- to sixty-foot-tall cottonwoods grow. They keep safe distance from the stinging nettles and seem indifferent to my rite of summer, like second cousins who attend the event out of obligation and are hoping for a good potluck afterwards.

After a few letters on the importance of knowing the unfathomable love of God, it's time for the tractor to move to another field and plow a different forty acres. The passage called the Road to Emmaus (Luke 24:13–35) is a good place to begin. Father Hewitt once opined in a homily that Jesus performed the mass on the Road to Emmaus. First, there was the Liturgy of the Word when he expounded on the Scriptures to his two travel companions (v. 27), and then there was the Liturgy of the Eucharist where he broke bread with them. After he broke bread with them, their eyes were opened and they recognized him (vv. 30, 31).

It is interesting to note that it was not when Christ discussed the Scriptures to his travel companions on the way to Emmaus that they recognized him. It is sobering to think that an expert in biblical studies can know more about the text than anyone and still not experience communion with Christ. I once met a renowned New Testament scholar from a prestigious and liberal divinity school and went away asking myself, "Would this guy even recognize Christ if He multiplied the loaves and fishes right in front of him?" Jesus himself lamented that the religious authorities of his day searched the Scriptures but would not come to him to have life (John 5:39, 40).

When you pursue the One Thing and experience communion with Christ, like the travelers on the Road to Emmaus, you will begin to see Christ more and more as someone who unifies and sums up all things whether they be explicitly religious or not. And, when you behold Christ in all things, you yourself will be transformed by gazing into his face. You will behold and reflect his glory:

> All of us, gazing with unveiled face on the glory of the Lord are being transformed into the same image from glory to glory, as from the Lord who is the Spirit.
>
> 2 Corinthians 3:18

There's a lot to unpackage here, but let's begin by saying that, in your Pursuit of the One Thing, you will more and more see Christ as the One who unifies and sums up (Ephesians 1:10) all explicitly religious or spiritual things. There are some elementary truths that need to be explored here that you may have learned your first or second year as a young believer. Please be patient with me as we start there and then move to deeper waters.

The communing Christian will see more and more how all Scripture testifies on Christ's behalf (John 5:39). From Genesis to Revelation, whether you are Protestant, Roman Catholic, or Eastern Orthodox, the Bible doesn't magnify a certain set of truths—it magnifies *the* Truth, Jesus Christ. Every book of the Bible either foreshadows, prefigures, or points to him (Old Testament) or explicitly reveals and magnifies him (New Testament). Even an Old Testament prophetic book like Hosea, which you may never have even read, foreshadows Christ's difficult relationship with his sometimes wayward and idolatrous bride, the Church.

Many biblical characters prefigure the person and work of Christ. Abraham is the father whom God tells to sacrifice his only begotten son (of Sarah). The commandment is cancelled when Abraham's obedience to God is proven. For the sacrifice, God provides a ram caught by its horns in a thicket just as Abraham believed.

Joseph serves as a type of Christ in several ways. Both are a very special son to their fathers, both are rejected by their own people, both are betrayed for silver, both suffer at the hands of false witnesses, and both, after humbling circumstances, are exalted to their respective thrones.

Certain major events in the Bible foreshadow the person and work of Christ. The Exodus (Exodus

12–18) and the Tabernacle of Moses (Exodus 25–40) point to Christ in scores of ways and the student of the Bible is encouraged to consult the vast literature available on those subjects and confirm what Christ said about himself: "In the volume of the Book it is written of Me" (Hebrews 10:7 King James Version)

In your Pursuit of the One Thing, you will behold Christ and begin to interpret the various doctrines of the Bible in a different way. The passage in 1 Corinthians 1:30 says: "It is due to him that you are in Christ Jesus, who became for us wisdom from God, as well as righteousness, sanctification, and redemption…" Wisdom is not a thing or a doctrine; Wisdom is a person. The same can be said for righteousness, sanctification, and redemption. Christ Jesus, *who became for us*. These are not individual, isolated doctrines found in some systematic theology; this is Christ, the Bread of Life, sharing himself with his hungry followers as wisdom, righteousness, sanctification, and redemption.

The heart of the Father is to put all things (including religious and spiritual things) under the Son's feet (Ephesians 1:22) so that in all things the Son would have the preeminence. Two stories from the Gospel of Matthew reveal this: The Baptism of Jesus (Matthew 3:13–17) and The Transfiguration of Jesus (Matthew 17:1–8).

These two stories have many religious layers and entire doctoral dissertations have been written about them. Yet both stories are punctuated at the end with the Father saying, "This is my beloved Son, with whom I am well pleased…" and the latter story has the important addition, "…listen to him." Peter wanted to keep the Feast of Tabernacles by building three tents in honor of Moses, Elijah, and Jesus but, at the end of the story, "when the disciples raised their eyes, they saw no one else but Jesus alone" (17:8). This is the Father's heart, in that, after we have encountered religious things in their myriad dimensions, we raise our eyes, and like the disciples, see no one else but Jesus alone.

When I converted to Roman Catholicism recently, a stunned friend, who I met in seminary, wrote me and questioned how I could do such a thing in light of "all the ritual and repetition, pomp and circumstance, and traditions of men in your faith that, like the Pharisees, 'tie up heavy burdens and lay them on people's shoulders…'" Instead of contesting every doctrinal difference we now had, I admitted that no religion on the planet had more layers or theological texture than the Catholic faith. I then added that "this provides ample opportunities for me to behold Christ in all the layers and texture, whether it's a creed, tradition, sacrament, or the latest encyclical from the Holy See."

I invite all of you in the Study Group to do the same in your respective traditions. Even in a church business meeting, you can behold Christ as Wisdom who helps a particular committee make prudential judgments in handling the church's finances. As mentioned before, when you behold him in the manifold dimensions of your faith, "you will be transformed into the same image from glory to glory" (2 Corinthians 3:18). Those who behold him will also reflect his glory. These are the ones who will strike gold on the Klondike, not those whose religions are merely multitudinous doctrines and practices that are disconnected from Christ.

When you look at the striking gold analogy that runs like a thread through these letters, you will see that Christ is the air you breathe, the water you drink, and the food you eat on the journey. He is also the gold or silver you find at the end of the journey. He is the alpha and omega and everything in between.

A delightful octogenarian woman who has been a member of my church for sixty years confirms the thesis that those who behold Christ will be transformed into his likeness. She has been a widow for about fifteen years but was married to a man who was not a Christian and very difficult to live with. She prayed the rosary everyday since she was thirty years old.

A major part of the rosary is meditating on different stories from the Gospels. Tuesdays and Fridays highlight the sufferings of Christ from the Garden of Gethsemane to the crucifixion. This woman named Gladys is convinced that by beholding Christ in his sufferings while praying the rosary, it changed her and gave her more patience with her cantankerous husband.

Be open to new exercises, practices, or disciplines that would facilitate the "beholding experience" such as contemplative prayer or going on a one-day retreat on a quarterly basis. Perhaps the disciplines you embrace now need to be revised. If the Bible study of a Pauline epistle is merely academic and generating religious information, it needs to be overhauled. Perhaps the study could be used to prepare you for communing with Christ.

The blast furnace continues here. I am grateful that it is a dry heat unlike the sauna I experienced in Florida at a conference years ago. My neighbor, Jim McAndrew, will be coming any minute to take a van full of people from Fawn Creek to Williams Lake to cool off. The air conditioning in the van is a special "four at 55" system: four windows rolled down going 55 miles an hour. The temporary discomfort is worth it for the relief we'll have in the cool, clear waters of Williams Lake.

The same blessing that God gave Israel I pray for you: "The Lord bless you and keep you! The Lord let his face shine upon you, and be gracious to you! The Lord look upon you kindly and give you peace!" (Numbers 6:24–26)

Under the Tender Mercies,
Uncle Aaron

CHAPTER 11

Dear Carson, Dennis, Greg, Paul, Bill, Alan, and John:

The heat wave has lifted and has been replaced by overcast weather with intermittent drizzles. This means the fishing has improved at Square Lake which is only four miles from Fawn Creek. Square Lake is generally a better fishing lake than Williams Lake (eight miles from Fawn Creek), but the latter is better for swimming, especially during a heat wave like last week.

My approach to fishing Square Lake is not as sophisticated as other lakes and waterways. The truth is, I'm not a very sophisticated fisherman, period. Father Hewitt, a pretty good fly fisherman, has forgotten more about fishing than I know. He outfishes me on a regular basis. He does graciously come down to my level by meeting me at Square Lake some early evenings as we try our luck with bobber, split shot, hook, and worm. This is my favorite kind of fishing. It returns me to my youth and the happy memories of fishing with my grandfather for bluegill and crappie in the small lakes in our county. There are no sunfish to be caught in Square Lake but, fishing for rainbow and brook trout (ten to fifteen inches) usually ranges from fair to very good in the mornings and evenings.

"The summer before I entered seminary," Father Hewitt remembered wistfully, "my brother encouraged me to reconsider my call to the priesthood and partner with him in a promising business venture. If I would've changed my mind and joined him, I'd be making six figures right now with a wife, a home in the suburbs, and, as a practicing Catholic, probably eight or ten kids! I'm happy in the priesthood a vast majority of the time, but days like last Tuesday make me scratch my head and wonder."

"It's not money;" he continued, shaking his head from left to right, "I'm with the apostle Paul on that one: with food and clothes, be content. It's the emotional wear and tear." My burly senior priest then recounted a brief financial history of St. Matthew's.

During the late 1990s, under a different senior priest, the church took out a loan for a new building to meet the seating and ministry needs of a growing congregation. On paper, the loan should've been paid off in five years, but then came the sex scandals that rocked the Catholic Church in the early 2000s. Membership and charitable giving declined a bit, and, by the time Father Hewitt arrived on the scene in early 2008, the loan had still not been paid off.

An economic recession gripped the entire nation later that year. As the housing market tanked, Clayton was hit especially hard because of its dependence on the building industry: from felling the trees to milling the lumber to building the beautiful, new custom home on the lake, many jobs disappeared. By late winter of this year, St. Matthew's was definitely running in the red and changes had to be made.

"I'd much rather have someone cut off my right hand or remove my eyeteeth than let someone go or cut someone's hours," the good Father lamented, "but I had no choice." The laying off of "the least necessary position" at the K-8 school and the cutting of hours of one church staff position from full-time to part-time, were protested loudly especially by the (former) school employee. "Perhaps one good thing that may come out of this," Father Hewitt opined as he took an extra-long drag on his cigar, "is that my time in purgatory will be shortened because of the pain I feel now." He laughed a laugh that was equal parts levity and anguish.

The last letter explored the importance of beholding and being transformed by Christ in what I called religiously explicit things: Scripture, doctrines, religious practices, creeds, sacraments, liturgies, etc. Again, the heart of the Father is revealed in the story of the Transfiguration of Jesus (Matthew 17:1–8). In a context with much religious complexity, Peter, James, and John, at the end of the experience, "looked up and saw no one but Jesus alone."

It's also important to behold and be transformed by Christ in what I call religiously *implicit* things. Now, we probably all agree that there is sometimes a false dichotomy drawn between the secular and the sacred. If, in everything we do, we are to glorify God, then every act is, in a sense, religious, and every moment is, in a sense, sacramental.

However, don't we all know on at least an intuitive level that there's a difference between me taking communion on Sunday morning and balancing my checkbook the next day after paying my bills? Or, look at another example. Paul, in your august Study Group, recently married Julie. Isn't there a difference between this sacramental ceremony and Paul taking out the trash the day before? If there's no difference, then why did Paul spend hundreds of dollars on a suit for his wedding, but took the trash out in his sweatpants? His dress matches the gravity of the occasion. I say these things in no way to demean the religiously implicit—in fact, I think there are many believers who need new eyes of faith to behold Christ in everyday life, to see him outside the four walls of a church.

Dear Study Group, I can make you this promise: If you set your heart to behold Christ in all things—the religiously explicit and the implicit—during your brief pilgrimage in this Valley of Tears, you will strike gold on the Yukon, you will hear Christ say, "Well done, you good and faithful servant." If you sit at his feet as Mary did, beholding him with reverence and adoration in the diverse contexts of life, you will reach your desired destination.

Such a discipline as this will inoculate you against idolatry. Idolatry means divinizing or having an unhealthy attachment to some created thing. Put another way, it means beholding and being transformed by that created thing. But how can you have an unhealthy attachment to Money, Sex, and Power or "religious idols" (e.g., I've known clergymen who were more enamored of the advancement of their ministry than their relationship to Christ) when you are beholding and being transformed by him? You can't. We should all pay heed to the last thing the apostle John told his audience in his First Epistle: "Children, be on your guard against idols" (1 John 5:21).

God has left his fingerprints in this world; his signature is everywhere. Beauty, Goodness, and Truth are what many theologians call the Transcendental Virtues. When you find authentic traces of these three virtues in sublime fullness, you can, with the eyes of faith, behold the face of Christ, because he is Beauty, Goodness, and Truth. This is not pantheism where Christ equals the created order. He stands outside and above the created order as an artist stands outside and above his painting.

This letter is nothing less than an invitation to the Study Group to become what I call "detectives of transcendence." These are believers who have had the eyes of their heart trained to behold Christ in the Beauty, Goodness, and Truth they encounter in the shoe-leather of the everyday, in their lives apart from church services, doctrines, and sacraments.

The Transcendental Virtues are like the Trinity in that they are distinct from one another, yet indivisible. When you have one, you have the other. They can't be cut up and divided like the parts of a chicken. For example, I have sometimes heard world-class mathematicians say that certain mathematical formulas, that obviously are related to truth, have a beauty and elegance about them. As the poet John Keats wrote in his poem *Ode on a Grecian Urn*, "Truth is beauty, beauty truth." Goodness is beauty and beauty is goodness. After someone has done a selfless act out of pure motives, a third party will often tell them, "You did a beautiful thing."

Beauty, Goodness, and Truth never came together in more exquisite fullness than in the Passion of Christ. The Passion was/is Beauty, Goodness, and Truth himself in his greatest act. Some in the Study Group may wonder: "We see Goodness and Truth in the Passion but Beauty? Where's that in the heinous reality of the crucifixion?" I call this "the horrible beauty of self-giving love" and we see this during the Holocaust when certain people risked and/or gave their lives out of pure motives for the Jews in Europe.

For example, during World War II, at Auschwitz, after three prisoners of war had escaped, the Nazi leader at the camp decided to starve ten men to death in an underground bunker in order to deter such escapes from happening again. One of the men chosen to die was Franciszek Gajowniczek who cried out, "My wife! My children!" In response to this, a Catholic priest named Maximilian Kolbe volunteered to take his place. When the bunker was opened up after several days, all the men had starved to death except Kolbe who the Nazis then killed by lethal injection.

Again, goodness is beauty and beauty is goodness. As detectives of transcendence, I encourage you to meditate on these things and also take some clues from these passages:

> The heavens declare the glory of God; the sky proclaims its builder's craft.
>
> Psalms 19:2

> Ever since the creation of the world, his invisible attributes of eternal power and divinity have been able to be understood and perceived in what he has made.
>
> Romans 1:20

A healthy ambivalence about the created order is understandable. I admit to being put off, after recognizing some atrocity in the human arena (e.g., greed, violence, treachery), some naive soul concludes how much humanity can learn from nature, particularly the animal kingdom.

A friend of a friend who is a cattle rancher in Wyoming had an interesting response to this fairy dust: "What am I supposed to learn from nature? That the strong will devour the weak, the sick, and the young who have been separated from the herd? That the female praying mantis will eat her male lover after intercourse? That the trained tiger in the circus will some day become untrained and maul its trainer to death? These questions don't come from an armchair philosopher; I see harsh realities like this all the time where I live."

Matt Paddleford of Cody, Wyoming, is anything but an armchair philosopher. After a decade of ministry and a particularly grueling year (physically, emotionally, and spiritually), the elders of my church told me (not suggested) to take a summer sabbatical. During these three months off, I spent ten days at Matt's ranch, a 10,000-acre cow-and-calf operation. I met Matt through a friend named Mike Daniels who grew up in Cody and now pastors a church in Greely, Colorado. He accompanied me in Cody.

One morning, over a hearty steak and egg breakfast, Matt, a widower, catalogued the last difficult six months of his life as a twenty-five-mile-an-hour wind blew outside over semi-arid terrain. Sage brush is everywhere and Indian paintbrush wildflowers are in full bloom. The early June heat is close to 90 degrees.

A harsh winter was hard on rigs and equipment and gave him some frostbite when he worked on a broken-down truck far from home. A heifer broke her leg and had to be put down. One calf was lost to coyotes. Last week, Matt had to cross the Shoshone River on horseback and said the experience "would put the fear of God into any man alive." Unpredictable cattle prices have caused him to lose sleep but he says he still loves what he does and wouldn't want to do anything else.

"You folks," I began over after breakfast coffee, "expose yourselves to things that the vast majority of people are trying to insulate themselves from. Take me, for example. My idea of roughing it is when I lose cable TV during a thunderstorm." Matt got a good laugh out of that line and then looked out his dining room window admiringly at the 8,000-foot Heart Mountain. "It's a good land," he concluded, "but it's undomesticated. It's a good land but it isn't always safe." And with that conclusion, Matt unknowingly planted the seeds of an epiphany that would change my life. I'll have to get to that in my next letter.

There's a flu bug going around both Fawn Creek and my church. I think I may be getting it because I have the beginnings of chills, aches, and nausea. I'm hoping I can sleep it off. Adios amigos.

Under the Tender Mercies,
Uncle Aaron

CHAPTER 12

Dear Carson, Dennis, Alan, Paul, Bill, and John:

What I feared came upon me. The flu lasted three days. I hesitate to go into detail because some of you may be near mealtime. It was so bad I can count on two hands the people I would wish it on: Hitler, Stalin, Mao, Pol Pot, Amin, and a few others. DeAnne McAndrew, Jim's wife and a dear soul, dropped off a pot of homemade chicken soup that saved my life. Yes, I exaggerate, but that's the way it felt on some visceral level. At the very least, she seemed like Simon of Cyrene to my Jesus or the Good Samaritan to my bruised and bleeding man on the side of the road.

To pick up where I left off in the last letter, Matt's words—"It's a good land but it isn't always safe"—resonated in my innermost being. Matt left and went into Cody to run some errands and I stayed at the house and wrote in my journal for three hours while I looked out at Heart Mountain. Through the created order, I beheld the Undomesticated God who isn't always safe. I embraced more fully the Christ-figure of Aslan in C. S. Lewis's Narnia series who is described as "good but not safe." In short, I received a theological education not from a tenured seminary professor, but, unintentionally, from a cowboy.

When I came to Cody for retreat and renewal, the formulaic approach to the faith that I described in previous letters—If I do behavior "X" I will receive favorable outcome "Y"—was definitely on life support in my life. My time in Cody pulled the plug. "It is a fearful thing to fall into the hands of the living God" (Hebrews 10:31) took on new meaning.

We don't cut deals with the Undomesticated God. Good parenting and consistent intercession doesn't guarantee godly offspring nor does religious piety guarantee physical health and financial security. There are few guarantees with Aslan this side of eternity. If there were, he would be safe; if there were, he would be like a celestial vending machine.

While Matt ran errands in town, I meditated on the Undomesticated God of the Bible who left his signature on the landscape of Cody. Cody is a good land but it isn't always safe for people like Matt Paddleford. God doesn't always conform to our experience or our conventions. He instructed Abraham to sacrifice his only son on Mount Moriah and withdrew his command after testing the patriarch's obedience (Genesis 22:1–8). He commanded the prophet Hosea to marry a prostitute in order to symbolize his own marriage to the spiritually adulterous Israel (Hosea 1:1–3). As God the Spirit, he is compared to the wind that "blows where it wills, and you can hear the sound it makes, but you do not know where it comes from or where it goes; so everyone who is born of the Spirit." (John 3:8) As God the Son, he made a whip out of cords and drove the money-changers out of the temple (John 2:13–17).

His final act was the wildest of all: after a heinous and humiliating death, he rose from the grave and appeared to his followers.

While I surveyed the beauty of Heart Mountain, my meditations became more personal. I realized I had domesticated God and, therefore, had rendered kingdom truths about him less wild for my own comfort and convenience. I kidded my mentor, Conrad Kersten, later: "If domesticating God was like training a dog, I'd be 'Best in Show'!"

First, I would encounter a truth such as charitable giving or, more accurately, the God of Generosity who did not spare his only Son. Somewhere in the process of studying, understanding and practically applying the new teaching, I would *domesticate* the truth, rendering it more manageable, comfortable, and convenient for my lifestyle.

There are some "wild" passages in Scripture about giving. Jesus commends the poor widow for giving all she had (Luke 21:2). Paul lauds the Macedonians for giving, not out of their surplus, but out of their poverty (2 Corinthians 8:1, 2). And, again, we have the unsurpassed generosity of the Father who gave his only Son for the redemption of the world. We have Francis and Clare and other saints leaving us examples of wild giving.

And yet, despite all the luminaries who had gone before me, I found myself in Cody still domesticating the truth. My record showed, in general, a generous giver, but, on occasion, God would call me to the wild giving of the Macedonians and I would balk. I've grown over the years in this arena, but being a victim of a Ponzi scheme hasn't helped. Financial issues never quite feel safe. Study Group, please pray for me. God has more to do in my heart here.

Aslan is not safe. Shadrach, Meshach, and Abednego knew this when Nebuchadnezzar threw them into the fiery furnace (Daniel 3). They knew God could save them but were ready for the opposite outcome (3:17, 18). In Hebrews 11, the author presents us with a biblical history of those people who have been commended for their faith. Please note that while some were honored for conquering kingdoms, closing the mouths of lions, and putting out raging fires, others were lauded for being tortured, enduring mockery, scourgings, chains, and imprisonment.

Using contemporary examples, your floundering business may end in bankruptcy despite your best efforts and fervent prayers. Your failing marriage may end in divorce even though you did everything you could. Your child, who has leukemia, may still die despite your all-night prayer vigils and fasting.

Philosopher John Hick contends that we live in a soul-making world—a world where good character is formed through adversity—and not an "all-my-dreams-will-come-true world." Dear Study Group, we need to disabuse ourselves of an insidious romantic idealism where life is marked by storybook endings, white picket fences, and balmy breezes. The landscape of Cody confirmed to me again that we live in a fallen world and challenged me again to face life as it really is and not how I would like it to be. The sorrows that have befallen me in recent years are well-known. Beholding Christ as I looked out at Heart Mountain—"He's good but he's not safe"—in some ways inoculated me from the bitter offense at God that people often experience who find themselves in a soul-making world.

What I've written here is nothing new. This barn has been painted many times over the years. On the Undomesticated God and the undomesticated male, I commend to you the excellent *Wild at Heart* by John Eldredge. In both his fiction and non-fiction, no one, in recent decades, has written with more facility about finding the God of Grace in everyday life than Frederick Buechner.

Buechner exhorts his readers to "Listen to your life." Put another way, when Matt Paddleford said, "It's a good land but it's not always safe," do we just hear the random musings of a world-weary cowboy or is there something more there? As detectives of transcendence, dear Study Group, listen to your life, behold Christ in the everyday, and be transformed.

In the Sacrament of Confirmation, the Roman Catholic Church teaches that the person being confirmed receives both the gifts and the fruits of the Spirit. The Holy Spirit confirms this person just as he did the apostles at Pentecost (Acts 2:1–4). The gifts are supernatural graces given to the person: wisdom, understanding, counsel, fortitude, knowledge, piety, and fear of God (Isaiah 11:1–2). The fruits are character traits produced by the Spirit: charity, joy, peace, patience, kindness, goodness, generosity, gentleness, faithfulness, modesty, self-control, chastity (Galatians 5:22, 23).

Now I fully realize that different branches and denominations of the faith have different lists. I'm not writing you to argue about who has the best list. The purpose of this discussion is not to debate the finer points of biblical theology; the purpose of this discussion is to provide a theological preface to a story I want to tell.

The summer before my freshman year in college, I worked as a laborer for a general contractor who was an elder in the evangelical church my family attended. That summer, he was particularly busy with two custom houses going on at the same time. My duties were cleanup, running errands, painting, insulating, and providing unskilled labor wherever it was needed. Let's just say I learned right away which end of the shovel to use.

One of the custom homes had reasonable homeowners and building the home went relatively smoothly. The second custom home had extremely difficult homeowners and everything that could go wrong went wrong. "This is the hardest job I've ever had in twenty years of being a general contractor," I overheard Ted Gregoire tell his brother at church one Sunday morning.

On the second custom home, because of a death in the family and prior commitments, the concrete company started ten days late. The usually reliable framing company had two new employees who were not up to speed. They misread the blueprints and took two full days to correct their mistakes. Then the wrong trusses were delivered to the job site. More time lost.

Ted had his (official) schedule and the roofing company had theirs. There must have been a failure to communicate because Ted ended up firing the roofing company and finished roofing the house himself. This was only the beginning of woes Ted faced that summer and fall on the Grayson home.

The Graysons themselves seemed pleasant enough at the beginning, but after the concrete company started late, Mr. Grayson began to micromanage every phase of the project. Ted received long lists of concerns and criticisms on a regular basis. He was sorry that the project had fallen behind and, with his subcontractors, worked long hours and Saturdays to catch up.

Some magazines portray homes having a glossy perfection. Then there's building excellent homes in the real world. The Graysons had all of the former conception of homebuilding and none of the latter. They were what you call "old money." Because they never did any of their own home improvement projects, they assumed, for example, that the drywall company could achieve the smooth perfection of countertops with their walls and not break a sweat doing it! And then they wanted Ted to do extras in the house that were not part of the contract, and do them cheaply.

Ted, for his part, stood his ground on items beyond the contract and was fairly remunerated. In revisiting the lists of the aforementioned gifts and fruits of the Spirit, everyday and almost in every way I saw Ted animated and imbued with a vast majority of these nineteen qualities. This is what many people call Christlikeness. After all, Christ was full of the Holy Spirit.

Ted managed to attain that delicate balance between being Christ-like and not being a doormat, between being wise as a serpent and gentle as a dove, and spoke the truth in love almost every day to Mr. Grayson.

For my part, I had just turned eighteen and did not recognize Ted's achievement. I wanted to tell Mr. Grayson to go play on the freeway or take a long walk on a short pier. I wanted to tell him to do things that are not fit for print. It was only later in seminary that Ted's luminous life dawned on me. I beheld Christ in that life and it changed me. I wrote him a letter just before I graduated and confirmed to him again, with gratitude, the old adage that imitation is truly the sincerest form of flattery. I wanted to be like Ted.

Again, as detectives of transcendence, we need to ask a similar question about Ted Gregoire as we asked about Matt Paddleford and the landscape of Cody: Is this just another general contractor going through relentless trials or is something more going on here, something transcendent, something Good, Beautiful, and True?

Some of you in the Study Group may be discouraged and think that you would've never seen these things unless someone pointed them out. Don't be. You're all young and have time to sharpen your eyes of faith to see the Transcendent. Even at my age, after decades of "detective work," I probably miss more than I see. Yes, there are days when I'm so spiritually myopic, Christ himself could be transfigured before me with Moses and Elijah on each side, and I'd be clipping coupons for my next trip to the grocery store! Perhaps that's what it means to be a practicing Catholic: I keep practicing until I get it right.

Under the Tender Mercies,
Uncle Aaron

Dear Carson, Dennis, Alan, Greg, John, and Paul:

A steady rain falls here reminding the residents of Fawn Creek that only five years ago our valley had the same amount of rainfall as Seattle. It's a good day to write letters and drink green and licorice spice tea. Lucy sits at my feet, resigned to the fact that her outdoor activities must be reserved for more clement weather.

A quart container full of clam chowder from DeeAnne McAndrew sits in the refrigerator ready to be heated up for dinner tonight. I sampled it for lunch. It's quite good. She claims her chowder has been upgraded in recent years with the addition of bacon. I can't make a judgment on that since I never had the bacon—free soup, but the batch in the refrigerator isn't going to last long, that's for sure.

On the phone, a couple of weeks ago, Carson mentioned that many of the members of the Study Group identified with the writer of Psalm 119:9 who asked, "How can a young man keep his way pure?" Or to frame it in a contemporary context, "How does a young man avoid sexual immorality in a sexually permissive culture?"

My first response is, "Why limit your question to only *young* men?" I may be middle—aged but I'm not dead. I still notice an attractive woman in the produce section of the grocery store. Sometimes it's both helpful and refreshing to get another perspective on a particular issue. Rather than tackle these complex issues myself, I thought it would be beneficial to turn to the wise and compassionate counsel of Father Augustine Lattimore.

Because of your youth, unless you are a film buff, you've probably never heard of Augie Lattimore, who long before he took his priestly vows, was an Oscar—winning screenwriter and director in the motion picture industry. His conversion story itself would make a great movie. Because his story and writings have significantly influenced my spirituality and thinking on sexual purity, I thought I'd pass some material on to you for your edification.

First, there is a piece from *Film Aficionado* from their "Then and Now" section near the back of the magazine that spotlights people who were once very much in the public eye, are no longer, and what they're doing today. It's written by screenwriter, film critic, and film historian, Heath Collins, a friend of Father Augustine's for decades, and provides a good window especially into his career. I found Collins' take on Father Lattimore's conversion and entrance into the priesthood to be both generous and interesting. It's always good to know someone's backstory in order to glean the most from their writings.

Second, I'd like to send you an excerpt from Father Augustine's autobiography, *By the Rivers of Babylon: My Journey from Hollywood to Holy Ground*. The problem is I can't find the book. I know that it is in the cabin somewhere but I can't find it. It's important because it specifically, though not exhaustively, addresses the question about sexual purity that Carson raised on the phone two weeks ago. What I think I'll do is send you the Heath Collins article now and then send you material from the autobiography in the next letter after I find it.

Here's the Heath Collins piece, "The Films of Augie Lattimore: How Augie Became Father Augustine":

"When I drove up to the two—story house in Westwood in December of 1980, the song 'Break on Through to the Other Side,' by the Doors, was blaring through the upstairs window. The house had quite a reputation and was called the Art House by students on campus. The student newspaper at UCLA, the Daily Bruin, even did a story on it and said that 'it was single—handedly bringing back to Westwood the halcyon days of the hippie crash—pad.'

One of the young men who lived there who was interviewed for the story said, 'It's not really a house; it's a facility. Officially only four guys live here but close to two dozen use the place. Most are aspiring writers, poets, actors, painters, sculptors, musicians who come to exchange ideas and perform. The Art House has an awesome synergy through a kind of artistic cross—pollination. And, yes, in one particular way, it's like Las Vegas: what happens in the Art House stays in the Art House. It goes without saying that no one who frequents the place will be entering a monastery or convent anytime soon.'"

(Maybe not soon but how about several years from now? I would've loved to play prophet with that young man).

As I entered the house to borrow an art history book from my friend Ted Gould, I noticed a fifth person had been added to the roster of official residents. With a sleeping bag and pad, he had taken up residence on the screened—in front porch. He sat at a card table with papers strewn here and there and maintained that delicate balance of someone who was obviously working on something very important but did not *act* self—important.

"Hi, my name's Augie," he said, shaking my hand. "Ted had to run a quick errand and said he will be back soon. He said your book is on the kitchen table. He also said that there's a cold beer at the bottom of the frig that has your name on it if you have time to hang out.'

Tall and lanky with jet black hair and hazel eyes behind tortoise shell eyeglasses, the first thing you notice about Augie Lattimore is a dignified forehead that would fit well on Mount Rushmore and an easy laugh of someone who didn't take himself too seriously. Ted's errand ended up taking an hour and Augie and I drank a couple of Molson beers and I found out how he ended up living on their porch. At the end of that hour, I felt as if I had known him my whole life.

After finishing a Masters of Fine Arts in Screenwriting at UCLA, he worked for a summer at a restaurant and then drove around the western United States, camping out and visiting as many national parks as possible. He came back to Westwood, got a part—

time janitor job, and worked out a deal with Ted and the other three guys of living on the front porch and working on a screenplay for $75 a month.

Since I had been carrying around a half—finished screenplay in a book bag for two years (which would eventually become the screenplay for *The Trials of Miles Campbell*), I was keenly interested in what bread he was baking in his oven. When he talked about his screenplay, I noticed he had genuine hope in his eyes that what he was working on could really be made into a movie. He said a director had shown genuine interest in the rough draft.

'Who?' I asked.

'David Ehrenstein,' he said matter of factly.

'David Ehrenstein! Are you kidding me?'

At the end of 1980, Ehrenstein was not the household name he is now, but he was well—known among film buffs and Hollywood insiders as a young director with great promise. He had one film under his belt, *Shell Game*, a well—crafted drama about a flim—flam man trying to go straight and reconnect with his ex—wife and kids after being released from prison in 1950s Chicago. The film was lauded by critics, had moderate success at the box office, and some players in Hollywood took notice.

Augie and I would drink many more beers and not a little hard liquor before he finished his screenplay two months later. He would then move from the Art House and share a two—bedroom apartment with me for a year. Ehrenstein loved the finished product, and with some minor edits, hoped to start shooting a movie based on Augie's script in summer after he finished his second film, *When It Rains, It Pours*.

Augie's screenplay became *Benson and Benson*, a comedy—drama about a college—age grandson driving his fear of flying, terminally—ill grandfather from San Diego to Portland in order for the elder Benson to ask forgiveness from and reconcile with a brother he hasn't talked to in almost thirty years. It was a fine debut for Augie as a screenwriter and sent a message to everyone in Hollywood that David Ehrenstein was going to be around for a long time. Terence Kiley, in the role of the grandfather, was nominated for an Oscar in the Best Actor category.

Augie would collaborate again with Ehrenstein two years later with the well—crafted and emotionally nuanced *Straw Man*. The two movies have the same cinematic signature: carefully drawn characters that you care about, witty dialogue that reflects the complexity of relationships, actors who inhabit their roles instead of playing a part, plots that have enough layers and movement to satisfy an American audience, and endings that have hope without being overly sentimental or implausible.

After *Straw Man*, Augie and Lauri Epps co—wrote the forgettable *Indian Summer* for director Conrad Schaff. Both Augie and Lauri would complain later that the screenplay went through so many 'surgeries' after they handed it to Schaff, that the actual movie bore little resemblance to the original script. 'When I went to the premier of the movie,' Augie told me later on the phone, 'I thought I had gone to the wrong movie!'

As good as his two collaborations with David Ehrenstein were, Augie undoubtedly would do his best work with Dick Broder in the film noir classic, *Perilous Times*. Augie loved the film noir masterpieces from the 1940s and had seen *Chinatown,* a 1974 noir gem, dozens of times. When we roomed together, he said more than once that someday he wanted to write a screenplay that would be like *Chinatown* with a happier ending, and he did just that. I'm confident that film schools will be discussing and analyzing the virtues of *Perilous Times* fifty years from now.

In the movie, based loosely on a true story, two bodies are found floating in the Los Angeles Harbor in 1952. The two murders take lead homicide detective "Pistol" Pete Yeager on an investigation that goes all the way up to the mayor's office. *Perilous Times* took all the best attributes of the movies with Ehrenstein and packaged them in a darker genre where life is cheap and almost everyone is for sale. The cinematography by Micha Krause, with its constant fog, dappled sunlight, and ominous shadows led one enthusiastic critic to rave, "*Perilous Times* is not a movie about old Los Angeles; it *is* old Los Angeles."

The movie would win Academy Awards for Best Picture, Best Director, Best Cinematography, and Best Screenplay. Augie was at the peak of his powers, and, to aspiring screenwriters, he bestrode the landscape of Tinsel Town like a giant. Six months after the Academy Awards, we got together at a party of a mutual friend and I was relieved that success had not gone to his head. Two things, however, had significantly increased in his life: women and Jack Daniels. The second I was immediately concerned about; the first I became concerned about when it threatened to end a relationship with the only woman, Terri Gold, that he ever loved.

Augie's experiences with directing received mixed results. His debut, *The Wisdom of Solomon,* was excellent and has aged well over the years. The screenplay, which he co—wrote with Ms. Gold, follows the romance of two Columbia University students from very different backgrounds— an Orthodox Jewish girl and an Irish Catholic boy— during the early 1960s. They will need the wisdom of Solomon to keep both of their families happy and navigate the tricky waters of an ethnically segregated culture in New York City. There is a particular authenticity and resonance in the film that undoubtedly came from both Gold and Augie drawing on their respective Jewish and Catholic upbringings.

This charming piece of cinematic real estate was followed by the forgettable *Hooper's Landing* that Augie wrote, directed, and had a small role in as an owner of a hardware store. It wasn't good enough to be memorable nor was it bad enough to be memorable and Augie later blamed the film's mediocrity on his undisciplined night life—i.e. drinking and womanizing.

Unfortunately, complete sobriety couldn't have saved Augie's next film, the abysmal *Industry Insider*, a story by a Hollywood insider about a Hollywood insider that was both a critical and commercial failure. They had to subpoena people to get them to come to the movie theater. Augie wrote the screenplay and directed a movie that couldn't decide whether it was a drama or a comedy and ended up being neither. The film had his characteristic witty dialogue but there was no chemistry between Cameron Bailey and Trish Santiago (they seemed like brother and sister more than lovers) and the plot meandered to a confusing conclusion.

I left the theater telling myself that that was two hours of my life that I could never get back. Many critics put it on their Ten Worst Films of the Year list. With the wretched *Industry Insider* following the pedestrian *Hooper's Landing,* there were whispers in Hollywood that Augie was losing his touch.

One month after *Industry Insider* had been universally savaged, Augie checked into the Betty Ford Clinic for alcohol abuse and years later gave an interview with *The National Catholic Review* about what happened:

'As I entered Betty Ford, three different traumas had converged in my life. I was addicted to alcohol, the only woman I had ever loved left me because of my drinking and infidelities, and my career was in a slump. I was raised in a devout Catholic home but I had put that all on the shelf when I went to college at UCLA. I went from being a lukewarm Catholic to a lapsed Catholic faster than you can make a pot of coffee. The three traumas broke me and drove me to depend on a Higher Power even though I didn't know who he or she was. It was like a Flannery O'Connor short story where a traumatic event causes the protagonist, who's been living in denial and foolishness, to come to his senses.

The year after getting out of Betty Ford involved a gradual return to the faith of my youth. It wasn't easy; I had intellectual barriers. God used the writings of

C.S. Lewis and Francis Schaeffer to clear away a lot of the intellectual debris that I had accumulated over the years. Funny how God used an Anglican and an evangelical Christian to lead me back to the Catholic faith.

My first confession after coming back to the faith lasted an hour! I had done a lot of sinning. I truly felt like a piano had been taken off my back. I started to attend Mass again and it became the highlight of my week.'

Two years after getting out of the Betty Ford Clinic, Augie's last film, *Olivera Junction* was released. Some critics called it a "Southwestern *Perilous Times." Olivera Junction* is not the equal of *Perilous Times* but it has aged well and excels in so many ways. In the movie, a dead body is found near the Olivera Junction in the high desert of southwestern New Mexico. The murder investigation leads Sheriff Hunter Stoops into contact with the region's Pueblo Indian, Mexican, and white cattle—ranching cultures. This makes Stoops, who is half—white, one—quarter Mexican, and one—quarter Pueblo Indian, feel like he is ideal for the job.

Autobiographical elements obviously informed the movie. Stoops is a recovering alcoholic going through a divorce and tells his deputy, "Drinking and divorce go together like Smith and Wesson." Hunter Stoops may be flawed but it's clear by the end of the movie that Augie wanted to present a Christ—figure who was destined to lay down his life for someone else. He succeeded masterfully in doing this without sermonizing or being didactic through Stoops' subtle gestures and every day sacrifices that lead to the ultimate sacrifice, his very own life.

Again, from Augie's interview with *The National Catholic Review:*

'By the end of filming *Olivera Junction* I knew two things: this would be my last movie and I wanted to be a priest. The scenery and landscapes and skylines of New Mexico spoke to me. You look out and sense the finite intersecting with the infinite as the cotton ball clouds move slowly from east to west across an azure skyline. The finite alone is not enough. I had had everything this world has to offer and the world was not enough. Romantic love is wonderful but I felt like I was done with that and was now more interested in a divine romance that coursed between me and the Trinity. I wanted the infinite and I wanted my heart to be a place where the finite (me) and the Infinite (God) intersect in a way that is pleasing to God who had done so much for me. I wanted to spend the rest of my life contemplating the Infinite and praying for people who had the same struggles I had in my Hollywood days. Perhaps this would be a good penance for me for years of a dissolute life.'

I've only talked to Augie on the phone about a half—dozen times since he went off to study for the priesthood. We remain on good terms and even joked about some of the crazy things that happened when we shared an apartment back in the early 1980s. Father Augustine Lattimore now lives 15 miles outside of Provo, Utah, in a Trappist monastery and embraces a mission of retreating from the world, living a contemplative life, and praying for the well—being of others.

I've heard from a mutual friend that he has become a baker and the monastery sells its famous ten grain bread to different grocery stores in Provo. The same friend tells me that when he's not praying or baking, he's working on an autobiography that he hopes to finish in a few years. I can't wait to read it.

More than a few people have told me they thought his career change "was a colossal waste of talent," and one said, "Think what a body of work he'd have by now if he'd stayed with it." The truth is that after *Olivera Junction*, Augie told me he didn't have any movies left inside of him. The tank was empty. What did he have inside him? What he's doing now. I'm not a religious person, but I do believe that if someone is following their heart and doing good in the world, then that's good enough for me. God (if you exist) bless Father Augustine Lattimore!"

I'll find his autobiography and get back to you soon.

Under the Tender Mercies,
Uncle Aaron

Dear Carson, Dennis, Alan, Greg, John, and Paul:

Hallelujah, I found Father Augustine's autobiography! It was in my travel bag that I took to Clayton a few months ago when I spent the night at a friend's house. It's interesting to note how contemplative prayer played a major role in helping both Sharon Houk and

Father Lattimore in their respective battles. So…without any further delay, here's an excerpt from *By the Rivers of Babylon: My Journey From Hollywood to Holy Ground.* You will no doubt see Father Lattimore's influence on my own spirituality:

"After my first confession in twenty years, I genuinely felt like a half—ton Steinway concert piano had been taken off my back. The peace that passes understanding flooded my life because I knew that God was now at peace with me. Mass became the highlight of my week, a grace—filled event that truly seemed to be where heaven and earth intersected and God and man communed. However, there were some trials and frustrations that accompanied those early years when I returned to the faith of my youth.

Most of my friends both inside and outside of Hollywood were "live and let live types" who said, "Hey, I'm not a religious person, but if it works for you, then more power to you." There were a few that were genuinely taken aback and critical and wanted to know why I had become a practicing Catholic. Before I engaged them, I tried to lighten the mood with a little humor by asking them, "So you want to know why I became a Catholic? That's easy. Have you ever seen the bishops, cardinals, and the Pope? What closed the deal for me was their hats and vestments. It's what they wear!" That usually at least got a chuckle and then I would also point out that I'm one—quarter Polish and John Paul II is also Polish and I couldn't resist the ethnic solidarity I felt with the Holy See.

So many areas of my life were transformed for the good initially that I started to expect that *every* area of my life would be transformed. My desire for hard liquor completely disappeared and didn't return. Friends told me that the underlying impatience and caustic humor that characterized my former life that had offended many people was replaced by a new gentleness that considered other people's feelings. The Golden Rule became front and center. There were definitely some verbal stumbles, but I tried in most instances to make sure that every word and deed was filtered through the question, "How would you like it if someone said or did that to you?"

Profanity and off—color jokes became rare. I had a genuine desire to give more of my money away to charitable causes and became more concerned about the poor and the unborn. I apologized to old girlfriends and lovers who I had used and I made amends with a powerful person in Hollywood who I had alienated by breaking a promise that I had made concerning a screenplay. And, yet, with all these good things going on, I struggled significantly with my sexuality.

No doubt there had been some encouraging changes in that arena. Before my conversion, my libido was like a slave master that had a hook in my nose and led me wherever he wanted. After my conversion, I felt like I was in a 15 round heavyweight championship boxing match with disordered eros. Most days I won; some days he won. Some people don't go from a libertine to a saint overnight and I knew that since his grace is amazing and his mercies endure forever, I would someday emerge victorious *despite* myself.

Anytime you write a book like this, you consider your audience and how it will meet their needs. What I write here will not address every issue every person has who is struggling with their sexuality. It will provide some helpful general principles, but someone who has a sexual addiction, for example, should seek out a professional counselor. There are many good counselors in this field, both Catholic and Protestant, who can help the sex addict.

Although I pray a lot for both men and women who have a disordered sexuality, I do have a special burden for men who are struggling with the same things I struggled with. I agree with talk—show host Dennis Prager that men and women fell from grace in different ways in the Garden of Eden. I think one of the biggest battles for women is submitting their emotions to the will of God. If the will of God is "X" and a woman *feels* "Y," her main battle will be to make sure "X" is done and not "Y." One of the biggest battles for men is submitting their sexuality to the will of God. If the will of God for the male on sexual issues is "X," his natural inclination is often to want to do "Y," and his main battle will be to do "X."

The recent findings of neurobiology bear this out. In her book, *The Male Brain*, neuropsychiatrist Louann Brizendine reveals that the human brain develops an area for sexual pursuit in the hypothalamus that is 2.5 times larger in men than in women. She also points out that the fuel that runs sexual desire is testosterone and men have 10 times more of this than women. Perhaps this explains why pornography and strip clubs targeting a male audience are dramatically more profitable financially than when these two things target a female audience. Yes, men have a strong sex—drive but more than that, men are *sexual beings*.

When this internal primal drive in men is tempted every day with the messages of the world, the desires of the flesh, and the enticements of the devil, it creates for many men their greatest trial. Forces from *within* combined with forces from *without* probably drove my namesake Augustine to say, "Give me chastity and continence, but not yet." When I think of what men (and women) go through on a daily basis and remember what I went through, it drives me to my knees to pray for them.

One day while deep in contemplative prayer during my time studying for the priesthood, I saw in my mind's eye or with the eyes of faith a sobering mental picture or vision. I saw a huge dam like Hoover Dam on the Arizona—Nevada border. Dark forces, who were out to destroy humankind, owned and operated the dam. Water was released in huge amounts into a large river. Boats on the river were capsized and people drowned.

As I meditated on this mental picture, I concluded that the river was Western civilization and what was being released was the floodgates of sensuality. The people being drowned were the citizens of this civilization. They were dependent on the prayers of the holy ones for their survival. These were people just like me during my Hollywood days. They needed someone to pray for them like my grandmother prayed for me. I've logged many hours praying for them. The floodgates of sensuality have many dimensions:

Scantily—clad women out in public. Women in low—cut dresses on magazine covers. Ditto for billboards. Late night talk shows that make deviancy the norm. Promiscuous women flirting with them at their workplace and vice—versa. R—rated movies that should be rated NC—17. Soft—core pornography that surprises them late at night when they're alone in a hotel room on a business trip. Polls vary but a shocking percentage of men and women, Christian and non—Christian, have affairs and are addicted to pornography. In today's world, monogamy and a pornography—free life seem like major accomplishments.

When devout Catholics read these statistics, they often hearken back to the apparition of Mary the Mother of God at Fatima where she told the child Jacinta: "More souls go to hell because of sins of the flesh [misuse of sex] than for any other reason."

My own frustrations led me to a counseling session with my priest at the time that culminated in this exchange:

'Father Zahn, the very things that the Catholic Church forbids—impure thoughts, masturbation, pornography, pre—marital sex—were like breakfast, lunch, dinner, and a midnight snack for me in my old life.'

'Would you like me to ask the Magisterium to change their teaching?'

'No, I'm just saying that the Catholic faith right now doesn't feel difficult; it feels impossible.'

'That's because it *is* impossible. But what is impossible with men is not impossible with God. The same God who delivered you from your alcoholism can deliver you from your sexual struggles. The first was almost instantaneous, the second will be gradual. You had to come to the end of yourself and depend on a Higher Power for your alcoholism and you'll have to do the same for this. Only now you have a name for your Higher Power: Jesus Christ.'

'Okay, in the meantime, I'll just get used to standing in line for confession every Saturday night.' The good Father laughed and I made my confession.

One of the good things that can come out of a long battle with sin are the lessons learned that you can pass on to other people. Notice the foundational lesson imbedded in my exchange with Father Zahn: *brokenness*. We must humble ourselves, realize we are powerless against disordered eros, and understand that apart from Christ, we can do nothing (John 15:5).

We cannot win fighting against a twisted primal sexuality, but we can win by letting Christ live and fight through us. We are very weak people fighting a huge problem and need a big God to intervene. We've trusted him for forgiveness of sins, guidance, provision, protection and physical health, and now we must trust him for deliverance from the paw of the bear— a disordered sexuality.

In battling a disordered sexuality, one of the obvious things that is so often overlooked is the importance of avoiding the occasion for sin. Another way of saying this is that you cannot sin if you don't put yourself in the position to sin. *You can't get eaten by a rampaging bear unless you put yourself in close proximity to it.* I'm embarrassed to admit how long this took me to learn.

For example, if you're in a restaurant and there is a very attractive waitress that is causing your mind to go places it shouldn't, then sit facing the wall. Preferably a wall without a mirror. If you have problems with pornography late at night on cable TV, then call the cable company and arrange your programming so it's 100% clean. Or forget cable and TV altogether. Do the same thing with the internet. Put filters on your computer that make it difficult for pornography to come in to you or for you to go to pornography. If you're traveling on a business trip, only stay in at a motel or hotel that has clean cable programming at night.

Sometimes you may have to end a relationship or get eaten by the bear. This happened to me about six months after I became a Catholic. I began to date a very attractive woman who I thought was on a similar path as mine. After several years in the fashion industry, she had become disillusioned with "Vanity Fair" and was pursuing a more spiritual direction.

She claimed to be a Christian but later said that she had given up on trying to abstain from pre—marital sex a long time ago because it was simply too hard when she met someone she loved and trusted. Physically, the relationship went too far. Way too far. She had a lot of wonderful qualities, but it became clear that I either would have to end the relationship or be "bear food" as long as I stayed in it.

Being accountable to other men for your sexuality is invaluable in the battle. Even now as a Trappist monk, especially because of my past, I'm accountable to another priest for my thoughts and actions in this arena. If I travel, I will call him and check in and he makes sure I'm staying on the straight and narrow. Men can get in trouble if they are away from home and have time on their hands. The old saying, "Idleness is the devil's workshop," didn't gain currency for nothing.

The primal sexuality within each of us is powerful and it's helpful to have to answer to someone else besides God: 'Two are better than one: they get a good wage for their labor. If one falls, the other will lift up his companion. Woe to the solitary man! For if he should fall, he has no one to lift him up' (Ecclesiastes 4:9, 10).

During those early years after I became a Catholic, I came upon a theme that runs through Scripture that provided a springboard for spiritual practices that would help me with my struggles. In Numbers 21:4—9 the children of Israel have once again rebelled against God and Moses in an egregious manner and God has punished them by sending venomous snakes among them. The snakes bit the Israelites and many died. The people regretted what they did and pleaded with Moses to have God remove the snakes. God then commanded Moses to make a bronze snake and put it on a pole. Anyone who gazed upon the bronze snake, who had been bitten, was healed.

In John 3:14 and 15 Jesus references this story and says, "And just as Moses lifted up the serpent in the desert, so must the Son of Man be lifted up, so that everyone who believes in him may have eternal life." I identified with the children of Israel because succumbing to disordered eros felt like getting bitten by a snake. The passage in the Gospel of John provided hope for me because it suggested that gazing upon the face of Christ could bring healing and life.

Other passages confirmed this theme. II Corinthians 3:18 says that when we gaze with unveiled face on the glory of the Lord we are *transformed* into the same image and grow from glory to glory. Hebrews 12:1 and 2 tells the battle—weary audience to put away their burdens and besetting sins and run the race before them while fixing their eyes upon Jesus, the author and finisher of their faith.

When I meditated on this thread in the Holy Writ, a number of things came to mind. I felt hopeful that, by the grace of God, I could exchange the pornographic images that plagued my mind with the wonderful and kind face of Christ; that in gazing upon Christ for long periods of time, there would be a giving and receiving of love between us that would transform me and conform me to his image.

As a person who came out of a Twelve Step program, I wholeheartedly believe in step 3 where the recovering person is exhorted to take a fearless moral inventory of their lives. Self—examination of our sins and weaknesses is crucial to personal growth. However, as much as I believe that we grow by taking a look at ourselves, I believe we grow significantly *more* by beholding his merciful and gracious face.

Contemplative prayer is central for me as far as *how* this is accomplished. Now when people hear the words "contemplative prayer," many of them feel intimidated as if such a practice were reserved for elite Christians, monks, clergy, and holy ones in the hushed tones of sacred settings. Nothing could be further from the truth.

When Saint John Vianney walked into church one day and found an old peasant farmer praying and asked him what he was doing, the old man said, "I look at him and he looks at me." That's contemplative prayer! Saint Teresa of Avila said, "Contemplative prayer, in my opinion, is nothing else than a close sharing between friends."

You can start this practice today. During your prayers, put a chair in front of you. Picture Jesus in the chair. He really is there, you know. Commune with him as two good friends would. Share with him your cares, hurts, gratitude, hopes, and dreams. He went to a great deal of trouble to secure this type of relationship with you by his unspeakably humiliating death on the cross. Therefore, pursue intimacy with him so he receives the reward of his sufferings.

What we do in contemplative prayer—behold Christ—needs to be practiced in every area of life. We need to see the face of Christ in our Bible readings and our bread—making, in beholding the Blessed Sacrament and the face of a vagrant, in a rural mountain landscape and in an urban ghetto, in the faces of our friends and in the faces of our enemies, in the arts and the sciences, in our greatest triumphs and in our greatest failures.

The Lordship of Christ means letting him fill all things so that he would be all in all (Ephesians 4:10). He is not segregated from any area of life. There is no Christo—Apartheid here, no Secular/Sacred boundary lines that are off—limits to him. He comes to us in the Sacrament of the Present Moment in every area of life with the Father and the Spirit, caressing us with his grace and mercy, disciplining us (also with great love) with his truth and wisdom. As we fix our eyes upon him and let him fill our lives, he crowds out our disordered eros and the snake bites are healed.

This is the invitation of the contemplative life. I found that the more I beheld the kind face of Christ in my life, the more my emotional needs were met. This is important because dysfunctional sexuality is often linked to unmet emotional needs. A person will often do some illicit sexual behavior to try to get love and acceptance that was probably missing in their childhood. But if we are being continually visited by the mercy of the Father, the compassion of the Son, and the warm fellowship of the Holy Spirit, combined with enriching human relationships, those needs will be met and we won't pursue disordered eros.

The contemplative life, in general, also increases a person's sense of the presence of the Trinity in their lives. (Some believers will experience the absence of God, or what is called "the dark night of the soul," but that's a different topic for a different time). This is a deterrent against participating in illicit sexual behavior. We wouldn't watch pornography if Jesus Christ was there with us in the flesh, and it's very likely that we won't watch it if we sense his presence all around us. An increasing awareness of his presence will often result in an increasing moral purity.

Perhaps the best advice I can give someone is not to give up. The oft—quoted passage, "For God *so loved* the world that he gave his only begotten son…," ministered to me. I realized that God passionately loved me when I was a pagan drowning in alcohol and promiscuous sex. Did his amazing grace and mercy end for me when I was struggling with sexual sin *after* my conversion? Absolutely not. If anything, he loved me more because where sin abounds, grace abounds even more. This love becomes a life—line that won't allow us to give up.

CHAPTER 13

Dear Carson, Dennis, Alan, Greg, John, and Paul:

Carson, thanks so much for your three-page handwritten letter that arrived day before yesterday. In an age of e-mail and text messages, there's something quaint and personal about a handwritten letter and the tactile pleasure for the writer of such a correspondence is often overlooked.

I'm blessed beyond measure that the ministry of Father Augustine Lattimore has been well—received and that you are all earnestly processing all that was written about him and from him. His autobiography has received mostly glowing reviews from Christian publications and has helped thousands of believers with different issues. I think that someday it will be ranked with Thomas Merton's *The Seven Storey Mountain*, one of the most influential autobiographies of the last century.

I'm gratified more than you know to hear that certain letters of mine have also helped certain members of the Study Group with certain issues. Early in my pastorate, when the church was growing and my name was becoming more known, I can clearly remember the Holy Spirit asking me before an important speaking engagement, "Aaron, are you here to *impress* your audience or *help* them?" The answer to this question will determine who you are later in life because we become our decisions.

I'm also delighted more than you know to hear that, in your last Study Group meeting, everyone now is more committed to become detectives of transcendence, to find God (Beauty, Goodness, and Truth) in everyday life, using your eyes of faith illumined by the Holy Spirit. You will behold Christ and he will transform you.

Dear Study Group, as many places as you find fallen-ness in the world, I believe you will find Grace all the more, because as the apostle Paul says, where sin abounds, grace abounds even more! Gratitude means praying for the former and giving thanks for the latter.

Carson, like you, I often behold Christ in the arts (literature, film, music, etc.). I own a copy of *Schindler's List*. I watch it at least once a year and never fail to be moved by it. Beauty, Goodness, and Truth come together in a cinematic banquet united by the story of Oskar Schindler's journey from self-absorbed womanizer to paragon of Christ-like sacrifice. When Schindler gives a speech at the end of the movie to the Jews he has saved, he tearfully regrets that he didn't do more. The Holocaust survivors near him comfort him with their gratitude for what he did do and I am reduced to a puddle: I have seen the face of Christ and want to be a better human being.

The question you raise at the end of your letter that concerns most of the members of the Study Group is an excellent one: As you launch out as a detective of transcendence with the purpose of seeing God in everyday life you may, because of the weakness of our humanity, become deceived and see God in places where he is not and be led away from sound teaching and morality? The answer to that question is "Yes!" and leads me to a story that has many lessons that are most instructive for those who are on their way to the Idaho silver strike.

Ten years ago, after speaking at a conference on the subject of finding God in everyday life, a good friend's wife asked to talk to me after the evening session. She was not a good friend like her husband but was more than an acquaintance. The denomination they belonged to was locked in a classic liberal versus conservative (traditional) civil war. The former pursued more of an emphasis on social justice and fighting the evils of racism, sexism, and classism while eschewing traditional views on abortion and homosexuality. The latter sought fidelity to what was biblical, creedal, and orthodox and endeavored to "communicate ancient truth in culturally relevant ways."

"Aaron, I really enjoyed your message on finding God in everyday life," Lydia, a pharmacist, began as we waited for our appetizer to arrive at a nearby restaurant, "but I think I probably apply what you taught in a way you probably don't agree with. Three years ago, our next door neighbors sold their house to a lesbian couple," she continued, her voice shaking ever so slightly, "and I've become good friends with them. I cannot imagine better neighbors or nicer people. I'm ashamed how the institutional church has treated such people over the years. It seems that 'Love your neighbor as yourself' is for everyone except gay people. Those bigots would be surprised, if they bothered to get to know gay people and ventured outside of their comfort zones, how much these people are just like them. They have the same struggles, hopes, fears, and dreams. Aaron, to use your own language 'I beheld Christ in them and was transformed.' I see God in them. They have more self-giving love in their relationship than many heterosexual couples I know.

"I know there seems to be biblical prohibitions against homosexual behavior. Remember, I'm a pastor's daughter. I know all the verses that are usually cited. I admit I haven't done an exhaustive study of the passages. I admit I'm following my heart on this issue so far but my heart tells me that the biblical prohibitions must be culturally relative. They must be related to a particular situation in a particular time but are not absolute for our time. I've come to the point where I doubt very much the Almighty looks down and is disapproving of what Kelly and Linda do in the privacy of their own bedroom in the context of a loving and monogamous relationship."

Lydia's eyes were somewhat hopeful when I began, "Lydia, I agree with everything you said," but then fell when I added, "except the part about those biblical prohibitions not applying to today's world." As a former evangelical and practicing Catholic, I have the same view I held ten years ago. This is rooted in a biblical imperative that is at least 3,500 years old, (Leviticus 18:22; 20:13), confirmed in the New Testament (Romans 1:26, 27), and buttressed by 2,000 years of

Church tradition. Perhaps more powerful than certain biblical prohibitions is the sacramental model set forth over and over in Scripture: "heterosexual couples in a loving, lifelong, and covenantal bond of marriage" (Matthew 19:1–12).

Dear Study Group, the preceding paragraph is actually a digression. The purpose of this letter is not to argue the case for heterosexual marriage; the purpose of this letter is built upon a particular biblical theology:

> But the serpent said to the woman: 'You certainly will not die!' No, God knows well that the moment you eat of it your eyes will be opened and you will be like gods who know what is good and what is bad.
>
> Genesis 3:4, 5

> The tempter approached and said to him, "If you are the Son of God, command these stones become loaves of bread." He said in reply, "It is written: 'One does not live by bread alone, but by every word that comes forth from the mouth of God.'"
>
> Matthew 4:3, 4

No doubt Lydia did see the image of God in this lesbian couple and was transformed by it: she became more respectful, compassionate, and empathetic towards homosexual persons. However, I think she went a step too far in concluding from her experience that Scripture sanctions homoerotic behavior. It doesn't. The most revealing words she spoke in our conversation were, "I admit I'm following my heart on this issue, but my heart tells me that the biblical prohibitions must be culturally relative." Judges 21:25 describes a time in the history of the nation of Israel where there was no king in power and everyone did what he thought best.

As detectives of transcendence who seek to behold Christ in everyday life, our subjective experiences and the practical applications of those experiences must be confirmed by objective, divine authority. For evangelicals, that authority is Scripture; for a Roman Catholic like me, it is Scripture, Tradition, and the Magisterium. The human heart is not a reliable guide to the gold rush. If it is not tethered by a source of divine authority, and we consistently rely on it, it will lead us to the Desert of Autonomy (Jeremiah 17:9).

Past letters went to great lengths to talk about the Pursuit of the One Thing. What we all need to be acutely aware of is that while we are trying to pursue an intimate relationship with Christ, Satan is single-mindedly pursuing One Thing in our lives: He wants us in an *autonomous*, rather than a *dependent*, relationship with God.

He wants us to follow our heart, do what is right in our own minds and reject the divine imperative. Lydia's departure from biblical teaching is merely one example of many. With Adam and Eve, the commandment was clear: "You can eat from any of the trees of the garden except the tree of the knowledge of good and evil" (Genesis 2:16, 17). We know Eve followed her heart and did what was right in her own eyes because the narrative tells us that "she saw that the tree was good for food, pleasing to the eyes, and desirable for gaining wisdom" (Genesis 3:6). The specifics of divine authority were clearly delineated for the nation of Israel in the Law of Moses, but, because there was no king in the land, "everyone did what was right in their own eyes" (Judges 21:25).

Where Adam, Eve, and Israel failed, Christ triumphed over the devil in his temptation (Matthew 4:1–11). Just like those who preceded him, Christ was tempted to reject divine authority and commit the sin of autonomy. Just like those before him, he was enticed to succumb to that sin in similar ways: the lust of the flesh, the lust of the eyes, and the pride of life (1 John 2:16). He crushed the devil's strategies and left us an example of clinging to God and divine authority by answering each temptation with "It is written…" Our only hope in such a context is that he would live through us and triumph again over Satan: Christ in you, your only hope of glory.

Dear Study Group, I have more to say on the issue of autonomy, but I will leave you with this: with all your getting, get humility. As I said in past letters, spiritual progress—i.e., making it to the Yukon gold strike—is impossible without it. Humility begins with the premise that following my own heart on a consistent basis will get me lost in the Desert of Autonomy. To use another metaphor, there's a reason Scripture refers to the people of God as sheep. Sheep are not smart animals. If left to themselves, they will get lost, be devoured by wolves and coyotes, and/or eat poisonous plants. Adios Amigos.

Under the Tender Mercies,
Uncle Aaron

CHAPTER 14

Dear Carson, Dennis, Alan, Greg, John, and Paul:

Only in a rural area. The evening after I mailed my last letter to you I got a phone call from Jim McAndrew up the road. "Aaron, we've got a problem," Jim began as I heard the disturbing and familiar sound of a dog yelping in pain in the background. My ears did not betray me. It was familiar to me because it was my Border Collie Lucy who was obviously in great pain.

Lucy likes to go up to Jim's house because Jim will throw his own tennis ball for her to fetch. She also likes to cavort with Jim's Newfoundland named Tugboat and play the role of the annoying, smaller dog that is "underfoot."

"Do you hear that sound, Aaron?" he continued. "That's Lucy. She got into it with a porcupine and the porcupine won. It's not as bad as it sounds. Tugboat had so many quills in him a few years ago I took him to the vet. Lucy's not that bad. Fifteen to eighteen quills total. You and I can handle this. You come up and hold her down. I'll pull the quills out with the needle-nose pliers."

After I arrived, Jim put on his work gloves and grasped each quill at the point of entry and pulled straight out while I held Lucy down. Lucy fought a little but then succumbed to the inevitable. Jim put a topical antiseptic on the affected areas and told me to watch for infection. We drank some excellent pale ale outside on his deck and listened to Fawn Creek sing its evening song. A chill was in the air and we both agreed that summer was definitely over. Lucy was back to retrieving tennis balls the next morning.

In revisiting the discussion of the last letter, I'd like to repeat myself: With all your getting, get humility. This attitude will provide a safeguard against the deleterious consequences of following your own heart or doing what is right in your own eyes. On our trip to the Nevada silver strike, this will help us not wander haplessly in the Desert of Autonomy.

Think of it this way: We are like a family in a covered wagon journeying from Boston to the silver strike in Nevada. Both the father and mother have a poor sense of direction and get lost easily. Both have never been outside of Boston and have no clue about the challenges that await them. However, they have plenty of money and can afford to hire a seasoned guide with thirty-five years experience of taking people to the western United States and even to the shores of the Pacific Ocean. He's faced every challenge imaginable and has never failed to get his client to their destination. He's the best there is.

We are like this family with a poor sense of direction. We need a Guide—i.e., a Divine Metanarrative—to show us the way. In relation to Lydia and the issue of homosexuality, in humility, we acknowledge that we are not smarter than the witness of the Old Testament

(Leviticus 18:22; 20:13), nor are we smarter than the New Testament (Romans 1:26, 27; Matthew 19:1–12). As a Roman Catholic, I acknowledge, in humility, that I am not smarter than over 2,000 years of Church tradition or the teaching office of the Magisterium. These sources of divine authority comprise a collective witness or Divine Metanarrative that, like a highly-skilled, seasoned guide, leads me to the silver strike and away from the Desert of Autonomy.

Though I vehemently disagree with Lydia, I in no way look down on her from the lofty perch of Pharisaical self-righteousness. How can I? I've visited the Desert of Autonomy myself on more than one occasion. The gatekeeper of this wasteland knows me by my first name.

In the early years of my pastorate, the church was growing rapidly and it became evident that we needed a building program to expand our seating capacity to meet the needs of new members. No one in the church at the time combined acumen in business and finance with biblical wisdom more than Frank Damone. He advocated a plan that was sensible, gradual, and would incur, in theory, very little debt. I distinctly remember him telling me, "Aaron, this is not a very sexy plan I admit. But the economy in this town is not good and will probably stay that way for at least a few more years. This gets us from point A to point B—unless the sky falls—without incurring too much debt."

Another group in the church supported a riskier plan that depended on rosy predictions for both the economy and the growth of our church. When the architect presented his plans to me and the Building Committee, I reacted the same way that Eve did when she gazed at the forbidden fruit: I followed my heart. When I saw the blueprints and the miniature of the building and dreamed of an expanding ministry, I embraced, and persuaded others to embrace, the riskier plan.

Three years later, with the church hemorrhaging red ink, I sat down with Frank Damone and only had six words for him: "Mea culpa, mea culpa, mea culpa." I knew and he knew that I had followed my heart and gone against clear biblical principles of fiscal responsibility. Much of this was rooted in my own hubris: "I can do things that other pastors can't do. I can circumvent financial laws that others cannot. I'm special."

Frank laughed at my "mea culpa." Fortunately for me two things happened: (1) Frank financially restructured the church and (2) the church continued to grow. Eventually, we were back in the black but I never forgot my season in the Desert of Autonomy. I know its arid terrain, cactus, sagebrush, blazing heat, and rattlesnakes. If we choose to *consistently* follow our heart, we won't make it to the Alaskan gold rush. We'll live in the Desert of Autonomy and you can't live in two places at the same time.

On the road to the silver strike, it's always good to have a seasoned guide who can read the weather and properly respond to it. The guide knows a violent thunderstorm is coming and it is therefore wise for the covered wagon to seek shelter rather than try to make it through Omaha, Nebraska.

In the same way, it is also good for the pilgrim and sojourner on the way to hearing "Well done, you good and faithful servant" to understand the *zeitgeist* ("spirit of the age") or cultural ethos of the time in which they live. What is the intellectual trend or feeling of the day? In the nation of Israel, the tribe of Issachar were endowed with an understanding of the times and knew what should be done (1 Chronicles 12:33). Jesus criticized the Pharisees because they could interpret the weather but didn't understand the signs of the times (Matthew 16:3).

Dear Study Group, I bring all this up because I am convinced that the present age is saturated with the message "Follow your heart" or "Do what is right in your own eyes." This shouldn't come as any surprise to anyone since that message is as old as the Garden of Eden. As the author of Ecclesiastes wrote, "There's nothing new under the sun."

The always-engaging Dennis Prager interviewed a twenty-six-year-old Swedish woman who was a student and told him that she thought belief in God and religion were ridiculous. Dennis then asked where she derived her values from and how could she determine the difference between right and wrong. She replied, "My heart tells me."

Dennis, who is deeply committed to Judaism and derives his values and morality from the first five books of the Bible (the Pentateuch), then asked her position on certain controversial issues like abortion and same-sex marriage. On every single issue, the student had an opinion and Dennis had the opposite view, because she was guided by her heart, and he was influenced by a divine text. In summing up the experience, Prager concluded that to follow your heart is actually self-deification because a person is navigating the issues and experiences of life with no higher authority than themselves.

The crux of this issue actually comes down to anthropology or, put more simply, whether we believe humanity is basically good or not. If humanity is basically good and, therefore, the natural inclinations of the human heart are generally benign, then following your heart would be a good idea because out of it would issue goodness. But, if instead humanity is a mixed bag of good and bad with an inclination to sin and even evil—i.e., concupiscence (Jeremiah 17:9)—then following your heart is a decidedly bad idea. The latter view is held by all orthodox Christians no matter what branch of the faith they belong to.

Think about what this has to say about the area of sexuality. For decades, the experts have been telling us how healthy and natural sex is. But, if we are born into a disordered condition, then is it possible, as C. S. Lewis asks, that many of the behaviors that the experts advocate (e.g., masturbation, pornography, premarital sex), and that seem to come so natural to the human species, may actually be disordered themselves? As I said in a previous letter, if 95 percent of the men I know followed their hearts completely in the area of sexuality, they'd all be Hugh Hefner!

As critical as I am of the "Follow your heart" message in the present *zeitgeist*, we all need to be prudent in assessing both the cultural ethos and individuals who are part of our lives. One significant characteristic of spiritual maturity is "having faculties trained by practice to discern good and evil" (Hebrews 5:14). Every time we hear "I'm following my heart," we should not dismiss it out of hand as spiritually corrosive. Sometimes, such comments are innocuous and even can be spiritually and emotionally healthy.

For example, it's innocuous when someone follows their heart and decides they like classical music more than jazz or earth tones in their home decoration more than blues and greens. I knew a young man whose parents were doctors and strongly encouraged him to pursue a career in medicine. He did have an aptitude for math and science but his dream was to become a world-class chef and own his own restaurant. He followed his heart and his dream came true.

When I was a pastor, I remember certain members of the church who were involved in certain ministries because they felt they *should* be involved in those ministries. Yet, when they followed their heart, they resigned from those ministries and did things in the church that were more congruent with their gifts and passions and emerged happier parishioners.

I'll be the first to admit that when I hear "I'm following my heart," "I need to find myself," "I'm doing this for me," "When I did this or that I felt alive," or when people emphasize rights more than obligations, my Narcissism Radar goes up and it's easy to dismiss it all as part of the self-absorbed *zeitgeist*. As a Roman Catholic, my general rule of thumb is that if it doesn't contravene Scripture (or biblical principles), Tradition, or the teaching of the Magisterium, I either support that person or assume a neutral posture of suspending judgment. Sometimes, those of us from "conservative" or "traditional" backgrounds can be too dismissive of a person or situation and thereby close off dialogue to secular people who may be otherwise interested in the Christian faith.

A few years ago, I attended a friend's wedding and struck up a conversation with a young man who was studying philosophy at the local university. He had enough tattoos and piercings for any three people. "I was raised in a hardcore fundamentalist home," he disclosed, "and got kicked out of Bible college my first year for drinking." His story went on to chronicle his alienation from his parents, friends, and home church and present experience at the university.

"I don't know what I believe anymore; I guess you could say I'm an agnostic on the big questions," he continued, "and it seems like when you get one question answered, three more arise to take its place." When it was time for me to leave, he said, "Thanks, Aaron. It was good to talk to you. You're not an A.G.E. Christian."

"A.G.E. Christian?" I asked.

"Yeah, that stands for Against Generally Everything. That's what I was raised with," he said, smiling. "No long hair, no short skirts, no makeup, no television, no video games, no movies that weren't G-rated, no card playing, no dancing, and absolutely no alcohol or tobacco. You were allowed to breathe but only on even-numbered days."

There's a good kind of "Follow your heart" and a bad kind. We should ask God for the wisdom to tell the difference between the two (Hebrews 5:14; James 1:5) so that we can avoid the soul- deadening landscape of A.G.E. Valley on the one hand and the Desert of Autonomy on the other. In closing, I'd like to offer some practical observations on the bad kind of "Follow your heart" and broach the subject by asking you, "What do you do when the whole world is coming down on you?"

I asked this question years ago to my favorite elder in the church I pastored. By the age of thirty, he had become a millionaire businessman and playboy. He lost it all but made most of it back by his late forties. In between losing it all and getting most of it back, he became a Christian and eventually an excellent elder in our church. "Before Christ," he began to answer my question, "when a business deal went bad and/or there were problems in a relationship and/or my IRS bill was triple what I expected, I was tempted by and gave into large amounts of good Scotch, pornography, and fast women."

"So what are you tempted by *after* Christ when the whole world is crashing down on you?" I asked.

"Large amounts of good Scotch, pornography, and fast women," the married father of two answered without pausing. "I'm tempted but, by the grace of God, I don't give in. Instead, I read the Word, pray, and fellowship with strong Christians. I'm accountable to other men like you for my thought-life and actions."

Study Group, be assured that we are never more vulnerable to follow the natural inclination of our heart than when everything is going wrong in our lives. It is not a question of *if* such fiery trials will visit you but *when*. What we specifically succumb to in the furnace of affliction often become our addictions or what the Bible calls idols. We tend to return to them over and over to relieve stress, feel good, take the edge off. It is important early in your Christian walk to identify and embrace those conduits of Grace—i.e., classic spiritual disciplines—that help you in a time of great testing. Return to them again and again and pray that they become habits of a holy life.

One cannot help but think of Christ on the cross. In the most extreme adversity, it would've been tempting to follow the natural inclinations of the heart and call down a legion of angels to deliver him from crucifixion and obliterate all his enemies. Instead, he was obedient even to death. Please, please know that when you follow his example, you are not just "getting through a rough patch." More than that, you are offering yourself up as a living sacrifice—it is an act of worship—to the Father who is well-pleased with your fragrant offering (Romans 12:1, 2).

> "May the God of peace himself make you perfectly holy and may you entirely, spirit, soul, and body, be preserved blameless for the coming of our Lord Jesus Christ.
>
> 1 Thessalonians 5:23

Under the Tender Mercies,
Uncle Aaron

Dear Carson, Dennis, Alan, Paul, Bill, and John:

Since my letters have been exploring the Desert of Autonomy and the perils of following your heart, I decided to send you this brief excerpt from Father Lattimore's autobiography, *By the Rivers of Babylon*, on how he went from a tepid Catholic to lapsed Catholic faster than you can say, "That's a wrap!" Once again, the sagacious Father Lattimore:

"As I said before, during my freshman year at UCLA, many things were undermining the faith of my youth: Darwinian evolution, being exposed to different world religions, my own youthful passions, and a desire to fit in head the list. However, it wasn't until I was in seminary studying the Psalms that the primary reason for my apostasy dawned on me.

One morning I read Psalm 84:11 where David said that one day is better in the courts of God than a thousand anywhere else and that he would rather be a doorkeeper in the house of God than dwell in the tents of the wicked. This may be one of the most profound verses in Psalms, if not in the entire Bible. In it David is saying that he would rather have the most humble place in the house of God than the highest position among the godless.

This is the exact opposite of what the character Satan said in John Milton's epic poem *Paradise Lost*: "Better to reign in hell, than to serve in heaven." What makes this passage so weighty is that it encapsulates the greatest temptation of created beings from before the creation of the world to the present day.

What temptation would cause Satan, an exalted angel who dwelled in the presence of the glory of God for eons before his fall from grace, to rebel and inaugurate his own kingdom of darkness? What enticement would cause a significant number of angels (probably one—third; see Revelation 12:4), who also dwelt in the exquisite splendor of God, to follow him in this rebellion? What temptation would provoke Adam and Eve, who lived in an Edenic paradise in unbroken communion with God, to disobey God's clear command and go their own way? What enticement led the nation of Israel, who had amazing supernatural provision from and a special relationship to God, to reject their Creator and worship other gods?

Satan, the fallen angels, Adam and Eve, and the nation of Israel all succumbed to the same temptation. It goes by different names but I will, for lack of a better word, call it *godship*.

Godship is rooted in pride, the root sin of all sins. Its nature is to make oneself God and to pursue an autonomous existence apart from God and his will. It means taking God off the throne of our hearts and, in self—exaltation, putting ourselves there. This is what Israel did in the time of the judges: "In those days Israel had no king; everyone did as he saw fit" (Judges 21:25).

This is what I did in my freshman year at UCLA. The name of the bridge that took me from nominal Catholicism to paganism is Godship. Many factors undermined my faith, but I clearly remember the weekend I decided to put my Christian beliefs and practices on the shelf.

All weekend long on television, a particular channel was playing Sergio Leone's spaghetti westerns over and over starring Clint Eastwood : *A Fist Full of Dollars, For a Few Dollars More,* and *The Good, the Bad, and the Ugly.* Eastwood played the "Man With No Name" who was a mixed—bag morally. He was definitely out for himself but was also capable of fundamental decency and loyalty.

What I found seductive was that he said and did what he wanted and wasn't beholden to some archaic religion that I felt was weighing me down with ancient rules and rituals. The freedom he had wasn't to be found in the Catholic faith or any Christian denomination. I would have to look elsewhere and the best place for me to start, I surmised, was my own heart.

Years and years of godship brought me to the Betty Ford Clinic and drove me to a Higher Power who I eventually identified as Jesus Christ. When I read Psalm 84:11 in seminary, the *why* behind my falling away became clear. David's proclamation here is a watershed moment because he is staring into the face of the history of fallen creation—a history inundated with godship—and saying, "I will not join the Rebellion. I will not commit the sin of godship. I would rather have the lowest place in the house of God than rule in the tents of the ungodly."

David would go on to commit egregious sins in his life (adultery, murder, etc.), but he was still recognized as a man after God's own heart (Acts 13:22). He would not commit the most egregious sin of all: godship.

Several times since my epiphany in seminary, I will get up in the morning, look in the mirror, and start my day by saying, 'Dear Lord, thank you for the gift of another day of life. By your grace, I choose to be a doorkeeper in your house instead of taking my fate upon myself. I reject the deception of godship and choose to be your servant.'"

Under the Tender Mercies,
Uncle Aaron

CHAPTER 15

Dear Carson, Dennis, Alan, Paul, Bill, and John:

This time of the year always reminds me of the passing of my dear friend, mentor, and spiritual director Conrad Kersten. He died when summer was over and the cottonwoods were just starting to turn yellow along Fawn Creek. As I said in a previous letter, he so incarnated the fruit of the Spirit—love, joy, peace, kindness, generosity, faithfulness, gentleness, self-control—that to use such words to describe him (e.g., "kind Conrad") sounded redundant, like saying "wet water." When it came to traversing the tortuous terrain of the soul, I had no better human guide than Conrad Kersten.

The last time I saw him, he had been a widower for a full year and missed his wife Ruth of sixty years terribly. Long retired from the pastorate and speaking at conferences, he was about half-finished writing his memoirs. We met at his favorite breakfast diner where he always ordered a vegetable omelet with hollandaise sauce and a fruit plate. This last time, as he walked into the diner, his own soul seemed freighted with a bit of melancholy. I wondered if it had something to do with Ruth's passing.

"This isn't about Ruth," he began in answering my question about his sadness, "though she is always on my mind. It's about something quite different. A psychologist friend once told me that I'm burdened with an exaggerated sense of responsibility and said he's surprised I didn't burn out in the pastorate by the time I was forty. He's right. The truth is I still fight the same battle, but to a lesser degree, as an octogenarian.

"Aaron, writing your memoirs is not good therapy for a man with my problem. The last three days I've been reminiscing about all the people I've known—and, yes, I remember every one of them—who began well in the faith but didn't finish well. To paraphrase from T. S. Eliot, they began with a bang but ended with a whimper. They left the harbor at full speed only to wreck their ship later on the shoals of human frailty.

"There's even a greater number of people who began in excellence but ended in mediocrity. They didn't apostatize their faith but instead exchanged bold colors for pastels and are now lauded by their secular friends as reasonable and in the mainstream. Aaron, I grieve for all these people. I don't beat myself up as much as I used to, but like Schindler at the end of the movie—one of your favorites, I know—I wish I would've done more. Specifically, I wish I would've prayed more for them."

In a definite role-reversal, I encouraged Conrad by asking him, "Was there ever a better pastor than the God of the Old Testament or Jesus in the New Testament? Think about the multitudes who wandered in the wilderness and did not enter the Promised Land. Think about how almost everyone abandoned Jesus at Golgotha. These two groups of people, the children of Israel and the followers of Jesus, had the best pastoral care imaginable and still many of them did not finish well."

Conrad smiled and gave me the look of a proud father to his son. "That's good stuff, Aaron. You brought you're A-game today, didn't you? And I guess I should be grateful for the scores of people I know who started well and ended well." I nodded, but, within a few minutes, the conversation magnetically shifted back to the fallen and the lukewarm and *why* they didn't finish well.

Conrad talked about Money, Sex, and Power and smiled, saying, "When I graduated from seminary, all the young pastors called it Girls, Gold, and Glory. Our professor of Pastoral Theology made sure we were very familiar with that part of Satan's playbook." We talked about the lust of the flesh, the lust of the eyes, and the pride of life for awhile (1 John 2:16). Then Conrad stopped suddenly, as if recalling a great epiphany, and said, "You know, Aaron, I've been surveying the wreckage of the fallen and the lukewarm for at least three days now and the biggest surprise in all my reminiscing is how many people didn't finish well simply because they got offended. They expected life to be X and when it turned out to be Y, they were scandalized." Like many times in the past, Conrad's comments served as seeds for further meditation. The harvest of these musings I now pass on to you.

> An offended brother is more unyielding than a fortified city, and disputes are like the barred gates of a citadel.
>
> Proverbs 18:19

> As a result of this, many [of] his disciples returned to their former way of life and no longer accompanied him.
>
> John 6:66

After breakfast with Conrad, when I did my own reminiscing about the fallen and lukewarm, his comments were confirmed by my own experiences. People are complex and the reasons for them not finishing well are myriad. However, in taking my own historical inventory, a number of offended souls came to the fore. When Jesus said to his followers that unless they eat of his flesh and drink of his blood, they have no part in him, *many* were offended. Remember, these were *disciples* and not half-hearted members of the general crowd who were hoping to see another miracle or get a free lunch of loaves and fishes. Additionally, once someone has been scandalized, either in their relationship to God or another person, it's very difficult to restore that relationship to its former state of health (Proverbs 18:19).

Two brothers leave Philadelphia for the gold rush in northern California. Fueled by romantic idealism and having no idea what obstacles await them, they travel about five hundred miles and are then afflicted by the three Ds: disillusionment, disenchantment, and discouragement. Both return to Philadelphia and go back to their former way of life. They tell family and friends, "We had no idea what we were getting into."

As mentioned in an earlier letter, romantic idealism is fertile soil for great offense. As John Hick asserts, we live in a soul-making world, not an "all-my-dreams-come-true-world" of storybook endings, white-picket fences, and balmy breezes. Aslan is good but he is not safe. Part of "putting away childish things" means disabusing ourselves of romantic idealism. A major aspect of growing up means accepting that we live in a fallen world: We embrace life as it really is and not as we'd like it to be. I've said all this before but it bears repeating because as someone once said, "Repetition is the mother of learning."

The ancient mind expected a difficult life. Jesus characterized the ancient Hebrew mind when he said, "Don't worry about tomorrow; today has enough trouble" (Matthew 6:34). Think about all the adversity Odysseus went through to finally make it home in Homer's *The Odyssey*. The epic poem reflects how the Greeks viewed life. Adversity was not a stranger.

Today, a young person in America can be raised in a suburban, middle- or upper-middle-class home during a time of peace and prosperity and be somewhat insulated from the reality of a post–Genesis 3 world. This is fertile soil for romantic idealism. When the true nature of the fallen world inevitably visits them, it's easy for them to be offended at God, life, and other people.

Dennis Prager on his radio show contends that people can often measure their level of anger and depression by measuring the difference between what they thought life would look like and how life really is. If the distance is great between the two, then the potential for both anger and depression is also great. This is one area where Buddhism and biblical Christianity agree in emphasizing the importance of having expectations that are in accord with objective reality.

The rain falls on the just and the unjust. Life is difficult for both the Christian and the pagan. However, the nature of the Christian faith adds new layers of adversity (and the potential for being offended) that the pagan probably won't experience. This is summarized brilliantly by Simon Tugwell:

> Christianity *has* to be disappointing, precisely because it is not a mechanism for accomplishing all our human ambitions and aspirations; it is a mechanism for subjecting all things to the will of God.
>
> *The Ways of Imperfection*

Put another way, the Christian faith—i.e., the Pursuit of the One Thing—is a place where our romantic idealism ("all our human ambitions and aspirations"), meet the cross of Christ. The message of Jesus was/is, "Repent, for the kingdom of God is at hand." It means that we will need to change our mind about many of our ambitions and aspirations and align our lives with the kingdom of God. Here there is great potential for Christ himself to be the Stumbling Block, because our romantic idealism often won't die on the cross without an agonizing, protracted struggle.

A friend of a friend was in the fifth year of his pastorate when he realized he had many of his "human ambitions and aspirations" wrapped up in his congregation. Because he didn't get his basic emotional needs—love, acceptance, belongingness—met in his family of origin, he tried to get those needs met in his ministry. He admitted to my friend, "I wasn't there to serve the people; the people were there to serve me. Instead of edifying or building up people, I was building my own little kingdom. It was a sick role-reversal clothed in sanctimonious language." The kingdom came in his life when three elders in the church confronted him about this role-reversal. Rather than become scandalized, he humbled himself, admitted fault, and began a season of personal renewal.

In recent letters, I've emphasized the importance in our journey to the Yukon gold rush of following divine authority rather than following the unreliable guide called the human heart. I encouraged the Study Group to think of this divine authority as like a seasoned guide who, for thirty-five years, has never failed to bring his client to their desired destination. Again, he's the best there is.

Imagine this guide, sitting down with you now, before the trip has started and telling you, as a Christian who is pursuing the One Thing, all the possible trials and tribulations you may encounter before you get there. He does this (and I do this in this letter) so that your expectations will accord with reality. This acts as a safeguard against becoming scandalized and returning to your former life. This was the apostle Peter's heart when he told his audience to not be "surprised that a trial of fire is occurring among you, as if something strange were happening to you." (1 Peter 4:12)

As someone who is pursuing the One Thing, expect a life marked by adversity because "it is necessary for us to undergo many hardships to enter the Kingdom of God" (Acts 14:22). You cannot be conformed to the image of Christ without significant and numerous trials (Romans 5:3–5; James 1:2–4). Expect significant persecution at least sometime in your life, because, as Jesus said, "If they persecuted me they will also persecute you," (John 15:21) and "…all who want to live religiously in Christ Jesus will be persecuted" (2 Timothy 3:12).

If you are pursuing the One Thing, those who are guided by the world, the flesh, and the devil will naturally hate you. You are a major threat to Satan and his kingdom. Expect demonic opposition. Expect to arrive at the Nevada silver strike with some scars. Like Jacob, you may even walk with a limp. These are not marks of defeat, but marks of someone who has stood valiant in battle.

Some may ask how God could allow all this to happen. God does not allow diverse and numerous hardships to happen to us *in spite* of his great love, but *because* of his great love. He wants a Bride, who, through much adversity, has been conformed to the image of his Son and is ready in every possible way (spiritually, emotionally, etc.) for the Marriage Supper of the Lamb (Revelation 19:7). We cannot share in the fellowship of his resurrection unless we have first shared in the fellowship of his suffering (Philippians 3:10).

It is common in Catholic tradition to hear the idea that Christ shares more of his cross with his closest friends. More than one saint has asserted that adversity is a gift of God and those nearest to the heart of Christ will endure the greatest trials. He holds his choice servants so close they feel his nails and thorns.

This idea is further supported when you look at the people who received the Stigmata throughout history: St. Francis of Assisi, St. Catherine of Siena, and Padre Pio of Pietrelcina are some of the holiest saints in the history of the Church. Rather than see suffering as punishment for sin as some "prosperity preachers" claim, the Catholic tradition claims that it often is a sign of God's love and approval.

"The grace of the Lord Jesus Christ and the love of God and the fellowship of the Holy Spirit be with all of you." (2 Corinthians 13:13)

Under the Tender Mercies
Uncle Aaron

CHAPTER 16

Dear Carson, Dennis, Alan, Paul, Bill, and John:

I'm down for the count. I overdid it running errands to get ready for winter and am presently assuming the "writer's position" or the "pray the rosary position." With two pillows up against the wall, I'm sitting up on my bed watching two strapping young men from my church stacking firewood on the back deck of the cabin. The cottonwoods along Fawn Creek continue to turn yellow and various maple trees, one here, one there, are not far behind. Fawn Creek's flow is down in its inevitable march to a frozen, winter silence.

You know my CFS is preeminent when I decline a fishing outing with Father Hewitt. He had good luck on the Columbia River fishing alone near Black Sands Beach a few nights ago. He caught three rainbow trout, all over fifteen inches, on a Panther Martin lure and wanted to meet me there again last night. No go. The only fishing I'm going to be doing in the next day or two is to reach into my refrigerator and pull out some tasty beef and barley soup and homemade honey millet bread DeAnne McAndrew dropped by this morning.

Carson, I appreciate your phone call two nights ago and apologize that I wasn't more helpful with your questions. I was exhausted and, as a result, long on good intentions but short on coherence and clarity. You ask substantive questions that are not easily answered in a sound-bite or religious bromide. Fortunately, in my present condition, I have lots of time and nowhere to go.

After the last letter about the perils of being offended, it seems that many in the Study Group are concerned that they may be offended at God and not know it. They're afraid they may not make it to the Idaho silver strike because they got lost in the Valley of Resentment.

My experience with people over the years is that often the very fact that they are concerned that they may be offended at God probably means that they are not. It's like a young man who came up to me after a conference and was very concerned that he was a narcissist like his father. Narcissists, by definition, probably wouldn't ask such a question. They're too self-focused to have any moral qualms about their condition.

The deeply offended soul wrote their own script for their lives but it didn't happen. They wanted X but instead they got Y. Instead of having gratitude for Y, they are filled with ingratitude and a strong sense of entitlement because they didn't get X. Often in the scandalized person, these two qualities so dominate that a voice in the soul that is present in the Study Group, that is concerned about offense and its consequences with God and people, is muted.

It's important to differentiate between "having it out with God" and experiencing bitter offense. A husband and wife attend a neighborhood block party and potluck where he makes a denigrating comment about her cooking. This isn't the first time and she's had enough. When they get home from the party, they have it out. The next day, he is contrite and makes every effort to repair the damage. The following day, things are back to normal and they make love in the evening.

Now, imagine that instead of publicly criticizing her cooking, the issue in the marriage is that he's an unrepentant, serial adulterer. They will have it out but it will go much further than that. Eventually, she will experience the three Ds—disillusionment, disenchantment, and disengagement. The marriage won't make it.

Now this analogy only goes so far because God, unlike the husband, didn't do anything wrong. However, the analogy is helpful in other ways. Old Testament figures like Job and Habakkuk had it out with God. C. S. Lewis had it out with God in his classic work *A Grief Observed.* They questioned his ways, but, as the narrative played out, God was vindicated, they were humbled, and a more intimate relationship developed between the two. This is what happened to me in the aftermath of my calamities. However, in the case of the scandalized soul, their bitter offense leads to deleterious consequences for their relationship to God.

As mentioned in a previous letter, the offended soul will struggle with the practice of spiritual disciplines. Spiritual disciplines—prayer, meditation, fellowship, Scripture reading, participating in the sacraments—are simply bridges to intimacy with God. But, if you are offended *at* God, you will not want intimacy *with* him and these spiritual practices will be grossly neglected. Jettisoning these disciplines is the sign of an offended heart.

The scandalized soul will also eventually return to their former way of life. After the children of Israel were miraculously delivered from the bondage of Egypt, they began to experience various hardships in the wilderness. Because this was not the script many had written for their post-Egypt life, many were offended and wanted to return to their former life under Pharaoh. They missed the fish, cucumbers, melons, leeks, onions, and garlics they used to eat in the land they left (Numbers 11:5). As mentioned in the previous letter, many disciples left Jesus because they were offended at the hard saying he gave concerning communion with him—"Unless you eat…" (John 6:66). They returned to their former way of life.

A story about a sister of a friend of mine provides a cautionary tale. "It's déjà vu with my sister, Aaron," my friend began as we sat around a campfire eating pork and beans on a camping and fishing trip. "Ten years ago, I can remember being concerned about her as I watched her going out to clubs with her girlfriends, all of them provocatively-dressed with heavy makeup. Now, a decade later, I see the same thing with a few differences. The girlfriends are different and I think my sister is trying to stay away from drugs this time around. Rumor has it she is moving in with her boyfriend at the end of the month."

The two "clubbing" images, ten years apart, are like bookends, my friend explained. The real story is in-between. "A little less than ten years ago," he continued, "my sister hit a wall, went through rehab, and became a Christian. She met a good man at church, married, and started a family. Almost from the beginning, a red flag went up for me because the operative word for her was 'exciting.' Her church was growing rapidly and that was exciting. The preaching and worship were some of the best in town and that was exciting. Her husband got a promotion at work and became one of the youngest managers in the history of the company. Yes, you got it, that was exciting.

"Early on, I sat down with her and tried to tell her that sometimes God does everything for us when we are young believers but then allows trials to come later so that we'll grow. We talked about the Parable of the Sower and the seed thrown on rocky soil. This is the believer that received the word gladly, but, because he had no roots, fell away when tribulation or persecution came. I looked into her eyes and said, 'Carmen, listen to me. Get deep roots. Get so tight and close with Jesus that when hard times come, you'll stand victorious. Today you have the tailwinds of success and excitement but tomorrow can be a completely different story.' I could tell she was only half-listening and felt a bit annoyed and infantilized by her older brother's advice.

"Aaron, I was never more unhappy in my life about being right about something. Because of an economic downturn and because her husband's company didn't keep up with changes in their industry, that company went belly up four years ago. He had to take a job making one-third less money. With their credit overextended, they lost their home and came close to declaring bankruptcy. Because of the stress, he began drinking too much and she had insomnia. The communication in their marriage, which wasn't good to begin with, got worse. Their senior pastor, whom she adored, was forced to resign 'because of the improper use of church revenue,' according to the Board of Elders. Aaron, I don't have to tell you where this is going. My sister didn't get the life she wanted so she returned to the old one."

A thoughtful review of this letter should leave the Study Group some things to ponder. If they're wondering if they are offended and don't know it, they're probably not. If they still have doubts, they should ask the people close to them what they see. Qualities like ingratitude and a strong sense of entitlement, two of the most repugnant traits in the human race, are difficult to miss. It's like my father used to say when a referee or umpire missed an obvious call, "Good gracious, Ray Charles could've made that call."

Again, make sure to differentiate between having it out with God and being profoundly offended. In the first, relationship is restored after an interaction between God and the individual. In the second, relationship is crippled. This often leads to an abandonment of spiritual disciplines and returning to your former way of life. From what I've learned about the Study Group, none of you fit this profile. Perhaps some of you in the last year had it out with God and wondered if you went too far.

The deeply scandalized soul is difficult to restore but not impossible. An offended brother is more unyielding than a fortified city but, remember, God brought down the walls of Jericho. Nothing is impossible with him. The anger the offended heart carries is enervating. Frederick Buechner is illuminating here:

> Of the Seven Deadly Sins, anger is possibly the most fun. To lick your wounds, to smack your lips over grievances long past, to roll over your tongue the prospect of bitter confrontations still to come, to savor to the last toothsome morsel both the pain you are given and the pain you are giving back – in many ways it is a feast fit for a king. The chief drawback is that what you are wolfing down is yourself. The skeleton at the feast is you.
>
> *Wishful Thinking: A Theological ABC*

The anger, bitterness, and resentment the offended carry is self-cannabilizing. This wears them down and even makes them more susceptible to illness and disease. Often people are restored because they are sick and tired of being sick and tired. They've drunk enough of the waters of Bitter Creek and spent enough time in the Valley of Resentment. They want to start the journey again to the gold rush.

I have more to say on this topic but will get back to you in a bit when I'm feeling better. It makes me smile to look outside and see Jim McAndrew throwing lime-green tennis balls deep into the woods for Lucy to fetch. She seems to thrive in the cool autumn weather and Jim is a good relief pitcher. It seems that our porcupine friend has moved on and is inflicting canine pain elsewhere, about two miles from here near the Gilbreth Saw Mill.

Adios amigos
Under the Tender Mercies,
Uncle Aaron

CHAPTER 17

Dear Carson, Dennis, Alan, Paul, Bill, and John:

There's not much new here except that I'm feeling better. Father Hewitt had to cancel a fishing outing on the Columbia at the last minute because of some undisclosed "emergency" in his parish. I went alone down to Black Sands Beach on the river and got skunked even though I used the exact lure the good Reverend used, and, to the best of my knowledge, fished the same stretch of water at the same time of day (dusk). Not even a bite.

With most of the firewood I need split and stacked, I'm more at ease about the coming winter. May God richly bless Clint and Mike, two high school students from St. Matthew's parish, for all their efforts. I'm especially gratified with the mountain of fire starter they stacked—dry cedar kindling—that's so good that a guy could use it and get a roaring fire going in his sleep.

Carson, this uneventful week has afforded me much time to both hurl tennis balls for Lucy and to think about many of the questions you asked in our last phone conversation, often accomplishing both activities at the same time. Lucy is definitely in fighting shape, just not with porcupines. My mind is also in fighting shape but my body often feels like it's had too many fights.

It's like a fighter who's past his prime, punch-drunk, and cauliflower-eared. He's got a new job as a greeter outside a Las Vegas casino and hopes people from his generation will remember him as the "contend-ah" he once was. I exaggerate here somewhat for comic relief and am truly grateful for my second decent day in a row after a bad week.

Study Group, it should be obvious by now that my heart for all of you is to develop a spirit that cannot be offended, a soul that cannot be scandalized. Two letters ago we explored the importance of having expectations of this life that are congruent with a chosen vessel of Christ living in a fallen world. No doubt the most significant bulwark against offense is an active Pursuit of the One Thing. "A mighty fortress is our God, a bulwark never failing," wrote Martin Luther in his famous hymn.

The Pursuit of the One Thing is just that: it's a following hard after an intimate relationship with Christ (Psalms 63:8) as an end-in-itself as opposed to Christ being a means to an end or ends. This is probably not a new teaching for most of you. Sermons, homilies, and songs of worship have emphasized "loving the Giver more than the gift."

In the New Testament, one thinks of the contrast in the Gospels between the people who followed Jesus in order to get their fill of the loaves (John 6:26) and Mary who pursued the only necessary thing (Luke 10:38–42). Then, there's Paul, who pursued the One Thing (Philippians 3:13, 14), standing in stark contrast to his opponents who were motivated by personal ambition (Philippians 1:17) and greed (1 Timothy 6:5). The latter made Christ a means to some selfish end.

In the Old Testament, we have David who declared that he only wanted one thing: "…to dwell in the Lord's house all the days of my life, to gaze on the Lord's beauty, to visit his temple" (Psalms 27:4). His spiritual DNA is the same as Mary's and Paul's in the New Testament. This is contrasted with the story of a young Levite priest in the Book of Judges in a time when there was no king in Israel and everyone did what was right in their own eyes—i.e., followed their heart (Judges 17:6).

This is probably an obscure Old Testament story to many Christians (Judges 17 and 18) but has been made more well-known in a famous sermon by Paris Reidhead called "Ten Shekels and a Shirt." In the sermon, Reidhead highlights the behavior of the young Levite who essentially contracts out his services to the highest bidder. In Judges 17:7–13, the young man agrees to be the priest for the family of one man (Micah) for ten silver shekels, a set of garments, and food. Later in the narrative, he leaves Micah for a better offer: the chance to be a priest for the entire tribe of Dan (Judges 18:19). In contrast to David, his spiritual DNA is more like Paul's opponents who were motivated by selfish ambition and material gain.

At this juncture in the letter, many in the Study Group may be wondering, "How does the pursuit of an intimate relationship with Christ as an end-to-itself function as a bulwark against being offended both at God and people?" Answer: If God or Christ is merely a means to an end as in the case of the Levite or Paul's opponents, then if that particular end (e.g., prestige, material gain) is not realized, it can easily become a cause for offense. Again, the person wanted X and was scandalized because they got Y. Their character had been exposed for having a utilitarian relationship with God—i.e., they wanted the gift more than the Giver—rather than possessing the pure heart of someone like Mary who only wanted One Thing (Christ).

It is difficult for a person who is pursuing intimacy with God to be scandalized. They wanted X and they will get X; they wanted intimacy and they will get intimacy. Christ promised them that. He said that he would be with them until the end of the world (Matthew 28:20), that he would never leave them or forsake them (Hebrews 13:5), and made these promises to his followers:

> ...Whoever loves me will keep my word, and my father will love him, and we will come to him and make our dwelling with him.
>
> John 14:13

> Behold I stand at the door and knock. If anyone hears my voice and opens the door, [then] I will enter his house and dine with him, and he with me
>
> Revelation 3:20

It's difficult for a David, Mary, or Paul to be scandalized because the script they wrote for their lives actually happened. They pursued the One Thing and got the One Thing. The same is true for today's disciples of Christ.

Though they did not arise out of a Christian world view, the words of the Roman Emperor Marcus Aurelius in his *Meditations* are wise: "Very little is needed to make a happy life" and "Happy is the man who can do only one thing; in doing it he fulfills his destiny." In many ways, Kierkegaard's *Purity of Heart is to Will One Thing* dovetails with all that has been written in this letter.

During my time in the pastorate and to the present day, sometimes I will meet a young, engaged couple and flashing red warning lights will go off. These lights tell me that it's probably not a good idea for them to get married. If I'm observing their behavior toward each other, and one or both of them communicate the unspoken message "This person will make all my dreams come true," it makes me question the wisdom of them getting married without some serious intervention from a seasoned marriage counselor.

It's not difficult to predict where the stumbling blocks of offense will occur in such a marriage. You will find them in whatever specific dreams did not come true. Perhaps she wanted an upper-middle class income and lifestyle and he expected an emotionally-supportive wife and willing sexual partner.

The parallels to our relationship with Christ are striking. We are betrothed to him (2 Corinthians 11:2, 3), have been given the engagement ring of the Holy Spirit by him (Ephesians 1:13, 14), and are scheduled to wed him in heaven at the Marriage Supper of the

Lamb (Revelations 21:6–8). Like a young, engaged couple, it's easy to have a utilitarian relationship with Christ where he is merely a means to our desired ends: e.g., good health, financial security, intimate marriage, fulfilling career, enriching friendships. Whatever specific ends we cling to become fertile soil for offense if they are deferred. If the offense is profound, it can consign us to a lifetime of squatting on Bitter Creek in the Valley of Resentment rather than making it to the Yukon gold rush.

The soul that cannot be scandalized resonates with the Westminster Confession: "Man's chief end is to glorify God and enjoy him forever." If a relationship with Christ that glorifies and honors him is the End, then we won't be offended with bad health, stressful finances, and a dead-end career. Some in the Study Group may ask, "Isn't it normal and human to want good health, financial security, a loving marriage, etc.? Where do we draw the line?"

This is an excellent question. Yes, it's possible to pursue the One Thing and have the aforementioned human desires. When a person with a heart like Mary (Luke 10:38–42) is unfulfilled in one or more of these areas, disappointment is a normal reaction, but that disappointment is worked out in the context of the Pursuit of the One Thing. A testimony I read in a Christian woman's magazine effectively fleshes this out:

"If I was to rate my marriage on a scale of one to ten, I'd give it a five," an anonymous woman wrote, "and, on a really good day, a six. My grandmother said, 'Our lives are like baskets. A happy life is a full basket; an unhappy life is an empty basket. Learn how to fill your basket.' Early on in my marriage, I realized that my marriage alone only filled about one quarter of my basket. My husband was consumed with work and struggled with depression. For a season I was crushed with disappointment. As a practicing Catholic, divorce was not an option. Neither was an affair. A wise priest told me, 'You need to figure out how you can get legitimate needs met in legitimate ways.'

"For starters, this meant spiritual renewal. Instead of praying the rosary sporadically, I tried to pray it every day. I read more spiritual books, went to Confession more often, and, along with Sunday mass, attended weekday mass when I could, about once a week. My basket became fuller though not all the items were explicitly spiritual. Christ filled me with things that did not necessarily have a religious label.

"I deepened the friendships I had and added one new friend: a self-professed agnostic girlfriend who introduced me both to the wonderful world of bird-watching and the wonderful world of wine and cheese sampled after the bird-watching. In becoming an accomplished baker, I got to return the favor as she sampled my eight-grain bread, apple turnovers, scones, and chocolate cheesecake.

"This girlfriend is counterbalanced by my devout Catholic girlfriend. We went on a pilgrimage to Lourdes, France, last year. If you're thinking our relationship is all solemnity, you're dead wrong. On the flight over to Lourdes, some things happened on the plane that were so funny I almost wet my pants! No truer words were ever written than the letter George Bailey (Jimmy Stewart) receives from his angel at the end of the movie *It's a Wonderful Life*: 'A man with friends is never poor.'"

The woman's testimony went on to describe other "basket-fillers," highlighting the joy of reading a truly excellent book, visiting national parks in the western United States, and taking a watercolor class. "To be brutally honest," she concluded, "though the basket is more full than it has ever been, I still have an ache for greater emotional connection with my husband. It's an ache that won't go away and yet I find God in the ache. Christ is there suffering *with* me, not taking the ache away but giving me the grace to bear it as he did on the cross two thousand years ago. The ache has become a friend and not an enemy."

When you compare and contrast this woman with the scandalized soul, both start out with legitimate desires. However, the anonymous woman has a relationship with Christ that is an end-in-itself whereas the offended heart often relates to Christ as a means to some end. The former *desires* a more intimate relationship with her husband; the latter *demands* it. The great psychologist Larry Crabb has written cogently in books like *Inside Out* about how the fallen human trait he calls "demanding-ness" can do great harm to relationships.

The anonymous writer's unfulfilled desires lead to disappointment but she works through her disappointment within the context of her Pursuit of the One Thing. She meets legitimate needs in legitimate ways. The remaining ache in her soul leads to greater intimacy with Christ. The scandalized soul's demanding-ness often leads to offense at God and people, and, as mentioned in the previous letter, often moves that person away from intimacy and back to their former way of life.

Study Group, what I've written here concerns two *general* profiles. Human behavior is very complex; this is not an exact science. For example, I've known Christians who became very convicted and sorrowful about having a utilitarian relationship with God and have moved into a new season of pursuing the One Thing. Because the Holy Spirit is at work in the world, that path—i.e., demanding-ness, offense, lack of intimacy, return to former way of life—is not inexorable. Don't be discouraged. As Father Hewitt often says, "You only lose in this life if you give up."

Grace and peace to you.

Under the Tender Mercies,
Uncle Aaron

CHAPTER 18

Dear Carson, Dennis, Alan, Paul, Bill, and John:

The splendor of autumn has arrived at Fawn Creek. The deciduous trees—birch, aspen, maple, tamarack, cottonwood—have turned or are turning color and season our valley here and there, mostly with yellow and gold and less with orange. The needles on the tamarack trees have turned yellow; when fall is over they will be a rich rust color trumpeting the coming of winter.

The water level on the creek is down significantly from spring. This has resulted in forming small pools and exposing heretofore unnoticed boulders. The ferns and undergrowth along the creek and in the forest are yellowing and old apple trees in the fields not far from the cabin have ripened and are ready for harvest. Snowberry bushes have lost their leaves and only the white berries are left.

In the mornings, our valley is filled with the sound of chainsaws and the smell of wood smoke from the day's first fire. Look up and you might see and hear the Canadian geese migrating to warmer regions. If you're one of my neighbors, you may also hear me yelling at Jim McAndrew.

In getting my car ready for winter, I tried to do one small job each day, Monday through Wednesday, because of my unreliable energy levels. On Monday, I changed the oil. On Tuesday, I did an admittedly homemade, not 100 percent professional radiator flush—i.e., the garden hose method. On Wednesday, I replaced a battery that had been deemed marginal six months ago. On Thursday, I drove my car up to Jim's because the retired auto mechanic volunteered to provide free labor for a brake job.

I love Jim to pieces but he often puts me in a no-win situation. He's hard of hearing but rarely wears his hearing aids. "A miserable nuisance!" he calls them. When we spend time together, I have to talk to him two or three times louder than the average person in order to communicate. Inevitably, Jim and I will end up in a room with good acoustics and I'll still be talking to him in a loud voice. Somewhere in the middle of my second sentence, he'll ask with a hint of frustration, "Why are you yelling at me?" Such small annoyances are tolerable when you get free labor on a brake job and excellent nut brown ale afterwards.

A major emphasis of the last letter was that whether we have a utilitarian relationship with other people (e.g., the engaged couple: "This person will make all my dreams come true") or Christ (Christ as a Means to an End rather than the End), whatever specific dreams or ends are not realized will often become stumbling blocks of offense in the relationship. What I didn't touch on in the last letter was trying to understand these dynamics from Christ's point of view.

Recently, I read an interview in a magazine with a man who is rich, powerful, and famous because of his success in the music industry. He's been married to his high school sweetheart for over twenty years and emphasized more than once that his wife is the best thing that ever happened to him: "She keeps me grounded in an industry of super-sized egos. The wonderful thing about her is that I know *she loves me for me.* She loved me in high school when I was in an experimental garage band that was going nowhere fast. Her father heard us playing one time and asked me, 'Is that music or did someone in your band just cough up his lung?'

She loved me just out of college when I waited tables during the day and played small clubs at night. Finally, ten years later, I was in a moderately successful band. We got out of debt and bought our first home. Then the band broke up over artistic differences. Six months later, I'm launching out as a producer and don't have two dimes to rub together. Many industry insiders are telling me the music I want to make won't sell. She loved me through all of that. The Grammy Awards that hang on the wall in my office at home are as much hers as mine."

Like the record producer, Christ wants a Bride who will love him for him. This is why he praises Mary in his exchange with Mary and Martha. She has chosen the one necessary thing and that is to sit at his feet (Luke 10:38–42). He is enough for her; her relationship with him really is an end-in-itself. Any blessings beyond that are only icing on the cake. Mary shares the same respective spiritual DNA with David and Jeremiah:

> You will show me the path to life, abounding in joy in your presence, the delights at your right hand forever.
>
> Psalms 16:11

> My portion is the Lord, says my soul; therefore will I hope in him.
>
> Lamentations 3:24

Someone in the Study Group may ask, "Didn't you say that we need both God *and* people? If God is enough, why did God say it's not good for Adam to be alone and then create Eve as a partner suitable for him?" This is an excellent question. The Genesis account makes it obvious that people need other people in addition to their relationship with God. However, another way of looking at it is to acknowledge that in both a sacramental marriage and/or a grace-filled friendship, God is filling us through our spouse and through our friend. I'll leave it up to the Study Group and the theologians to wrestle with these mysteries.

If you look at the heart of Mary, David, and Jeremiah and feel woefully inadequate, you're not alone. When I was about your age in seminary and would encounter great souls in the Bible, church history, or in real life, I definitely felt like I was playing for the junior varsity. To use the terminology of recent letters, I thought I was the quintessential mixed bag: equal parts devout and utilitarian, desiring and demanding, grateful and ungrateful, unassuming and entitled, like Mary but also like members of the crowd who were offended and returned to their former way of life (John 6:66).

In short, like Bunyan's *Pilgrim's Progress* but also like Lewis's *Pilgrim's Regress*. Here are some helpful signposts this pilgrim encountered along the way:

Christ not only wants a relationship with his Bride that is an end-in-itself; He deserves it. Remember that humility isn't groveling; it's merely an appropriate response to objective reality. Objective reality tells us that if not for God, we wouldn't even exist. "In him we live and move and have our being" (Acts 17:28). He not only is completely responsible for our physical existence but also for our subsequent spiritual, "new creation" (2 Corinthians 5:17). He endured an unspeakably heinous death to purchase our redemption and give us eternal life. We were Satan's slave and now we are Christ's (1 Peter 1:18, 19). We may be beset by adversity now, but we are blessed in heavenly places and have a future of the Beatific Vision—i.e., being united with Christ in boundless Beauty, Goodness, and Truth forever. No wonder a countless number of creatures in heaven sing, "Worthy is the Lamb that was slain to receive power and riches, wisdom and strength, honor and glory and blessing" (Revelation 4:12).

The proper response to God's work of creation and redemption is submission, humility, gratitude, and adoration—i.e., worship. The proper role of the person responding is that of a slave of Jesus Christ. This is why Paul often refers to himself as a slave (Greek: *doulos*) or bondservant of Christ (Romans 1:1). When you put the two together, the role and the response, you have a slave of Christ who worships the Lamb. This was an important signpost for me because it defined the journey: from quintessential mixed bag to adoring bondservant of Christ. It's a sojourn that is propelled by the Pursuit of the One Thing and ends in a gold rush.

Perhaps this was a precursor to my later conversion to Roman Catholicism but upon being gripped by the vision of this journey, it seemed fitting to perform some ritual that demonstrated my commitment to becoming an adoring bondservant of Christ. Some ceremony should reflect my covenant with God in response to his wondrous acts of creation and redemption. This became a second signpost and the story of Abraham and the Sacrifice of Isaac (Genesis 22:1–18) became its central text.

There were a lot of campsites available at Diamond Lake. It was late autumn and few people wanted to be there to brace the early night fall, cold nights, and half-frozen water containers in the morning. A full harvest moon and a good Coleman lantern made the nightfall less daunting. I made a medium-sized fire and heated up a small amount of chicken noodle soup. I was on a partial fast and wanted spiritual clarity for the long night ahead.

After dinner, I cleared and cleaned my dishes and kept the fire going with wood I borrowed from a neighbor. Each piece of wood represented an "Isaac" I was offering up to God as a sacrifice of something in my life that was very dear to me. Remember, Abraham was justified before God for his willingness to sacrifice what was dearest to him: his beloved, only begotten son of Sarah. Saul, in contrast, was sharply rebuked by God through Samuel for not "sacrificing" the best of the

Amalekites. He spared their king along with the best of their sheep, oxen, and lambs (1 Samuel 15:1-23).

A slave of Christ has no rights and no possessions. "The earth is the Lord's and all it holds, the world and those who live there" (Psalms 24:1). We were purchased by Christ, not with gold or silver, but with his precious blood (1 Peter 1:18, 19). To humbly offer what was dearest to me acknowledges this master-slave relationship and is an act of worship, each log on the fire being like a burnt offering whose sweet aroma ascends to the very Throne of God. Each sacrifice reminds me that everything is truly owned by God; everything we think we possess is merely on loan.

The first log ("Isaac") to be thrown on the fire represented my relationship to Claire (Jeremy would be born two years later) at a time when we were enjoying the first blush of nuptial bliss. As the log burned, I acknowledged that Claire was God's and not mine. I promised to always try to have him reigning on the throne of my heart and not Claire in his place. God would be my primary source of joy and happiness, while all other relationships, no matter how precious, would be secondary resources. And if the relationship should become profoundly disappointing, and even, for whatever reason, dissolve, I will find God in the disappointment and not return to my former way of life as a scandalized soul. All of these aspirations are not above and beyond the call of duty, but are merely the fitting response to God's work of creation and redemption in our lives. As Nicholas Ludwig von Zinzendorf, the founder of Moravian Missions, said, "The Lamb is worthy to receive the reward of his sufferings."

Several more logs were burned before I climbed into my sleeping bag at 2 a.m. These "Isaacs" included our future family, ministry, financial security, health, friendships, etc. I would encounter a third signpost on my journey from "quintessential mixed bag" to "slave of Christ who worships the Lamb" and that would be a vision of how to live out the content of my ritual in the shoe-leather of daily life. The letters you have received from me are permeated with that project and will take the rest of my life to realize. Yes, I think it will take a lifetime for this worm to become a butterfly, this lump of coal to become a diamond, and this ugly duckling to become a swan. Please take encouragement in my struggles.

Carson recently told me that at least two and maybe three members of the Study Group are seriously considering going to seminary after they finish their master's degree. This principle of laying our "Isaacs" on the altar couldn't be more relevant for those contemplating an ecclesial future.

As mentioned in an earlier letter, sometimes people go into ministry or priestly vocation who didn't get their emotional needs met in their families of origin. They then choose to use their ministry to get those needs met and a toxic role-reversal takes place. Rather than being there to serve the people, the people are there to serve them. Rather than being there to build people up in the faith, they're there to build their own little kingdom. Often, these men of the cloth must control and micromanage everything because God forbid if their precious "Isaac" is diminished in any way. In order to determine if you've placed your "Isaac" on the altar or not, ask yourself this question, "Can I walk away from this ministry and still be happy?"

Father Hewitt told me a story about a priest who had an international teaching ministry, and, while communing before the Blessed Sacrament one day, the Holy Spirit asked him, "Could you walk away from this ministry and go be an obscure priest at some leper colony out in the middle of nowhere?" The priest answered, "Heck, no, I'm having too much fun!" Then the Holy Spirit answered back, "Then you need to take a hiatus from this ministry until you can walk away. " The crestfallen priest took six months off and learned to lay his "Isaac" on the altar.

This question, "Can you walk away?" should be asked by everyone, whether they are successful in ministry or have had a meteoric rise in a Manhattan advertising agency. My experience tells me that the ones who can walk away are the ones who have embraced "My portion is the Lord, says my soul; therefore will I hope in him" (Lamentations 3:24). In reiterating a theme of a past letter, because they are getting their needs for love, acceptance, and belonging-ness met through their relationship with God and people, they don't need to get those needs met through their ministry or career and can lay their "Isaac" on the altar. And, yes, they will make it to the Idaho silver strike.

Not long ago, Dee Anne McAndrew told me she thought I was looking too skinny. Since then, she's dropped off beef stroganoff, shrimp fettuccine, and caramel pecan cheesecake. I appreciate her concern and thoughtfulness more than she will ever know but after those three "aorta staplers," I half expect her to want to hook me up to an intravenous feeding of alfredo sauce while I sleep at night. I have put on five pounds since her concern was disclosed so maybe she'll mix in a salad once in awhile.

Grace and peace to you.

Under the Tender Mercies,
Uncle Aaron

CHAPTER 19

Dear Carson, Dennis, Alan, Paul, Bill, and John:

If, as a previous letter suggested, my rite of summer is a ceremonial "baptism" in Fawn Creek on the hottest days of the year, then my rite of autumn must be my annual visit from Karl Stonegaard. For the third year in a row, he has come to the cabin for a three-day and three-night stay during the first week of October.

I pick him up at the Spokane airport on Thursday night and drop him off on Sunday night. In between, we fish, fellowship, smoke cigars, hoist a few pale ales, grill some steaks, and play cards with Father Hewitt and a friend or two from St. Matthew's. Karl, an Anglican and C. S. Lewis aficionado, likes to walk alone and pray early in the morning on the roads and trails near Fawn Creek "until I find my soul again," he says.

We became friends in college and were roommates our freshman year. After college, he graduated from the University of Michigan Law School and went on to a successful career as a tax lawyer and CPA. Karl is a man of extremes in at least one way: he's the worst fisherman I know but the best card player. When the first activity is followed by the second, he goes from strike out to homerun and from outhouse to penthouse. With typical self-deprecating humor, Karl, in a reference to his national heritage, said recently, "When I play cards, I'm the Great Dane. When I fish, I am the Great Pain."

After I removed his Panther Martin lure from my right bicep after one of his errant casts, I can attest that the second moniker, the Great Pain, is empirically verifiable. Apparently, they didn't have classes on proper spin-casting techniques at Michigan Law School. When Karl visits me, he often volunteers to pay for all the groceries. Sometimes, when we fish together with Father Hewitt, I seriously think about also asking him for combat pay.

As a card player, Karl is typical of many high IQ people with amazing memories. If success in a particular game is related to remembering what cards have already been played and predicting what cards are about to be dealt, Karl beats me, Father Hewitt, and whoever else, like a drum. He has never taken his "act" to Vegas and has been unsuccessfully recruited by others to go there several times.

In Karl's most recent visit, Father Hewitt and I wanted to provide him with an outing that really would be "like shooting fish in a barrel." Lindsay Lake, one of the best-kept secrets in Stevens County, turned out to be our "barrel." A parishioner at St. Matthew's, who owns a lakefront lot there, told the good Reverend that anyone could catch fish in the morning or evening, where Wolf Creek flows into the lake. The hot tip turned out to be understated. Pan-sized brook trout practically jumped into our nets. People sometimes joke that in a fraudulent political election, dead people end up voting for the winning candidate. Well, I'm convinced those same dead people could catch fish at Lindsay Lake. Simply exhume the bodies from the cemetery, put a fishing pole in their hands, and watch out. We put a smile on Karl's face. He texted a photo of himself from his phone to his wife with three fish he had caught on a stringer. His message to his wife read: "Next career: Fishing guide."

Dear Study Group, though sprinkled with humor here and there, the last letter was a weighty meditation ending with the call to be willing to put all our "Isaacs" on the altar. One concern I have is that with the cumulative weight of all the letters I've sent over the weeks and months, some in the group may feel like they have 252 new things to do. Remember what Jesus told Mary and Martha: Only one thing was necessary.

In relation to the issue of overcoming particular sins (e.g., anger, lust, sloth, envy, gluttony, etc.), think of the Pursuit of the One Thing as analogous to draining the proverbial swamp to rid the area of malaria-carrying mosquitoes. The Pursuit is the draining action, the mosquitoes are the particular sins one may be battling. As mentioned in a previous letter, if a person is beholding Christ, they will be transformed from glory to glory and are, in many ways, inoculated from idolatry (2 Corinthians 3:18). They can't behold Christ and an idol at the same time.

The last letter explored how when we pursue the One Thing and behold Christ as Creator and Redeemer, a new humility and gratitude transforms and leads us to follow Abraham in our willingness to sacrifice what's most precious to us to God. There's more ground to plow here, especially in the soil of seeing life through the prism of humility and gratitude. We'll be getting into what some people call Big Think: the exercise of taking complex reality and reducing it to a simplified form. Simplified but not simplistic. Einstein did this when he reduced complex phenomena to $e=mc^2$. But please don't think of me as a theological Einstein. You can do that with the apostle Paul, Augustine, Aquinas, C. S. Lewis, G. K. Chesterton, Hans von Balthasar, Karl Barth, et al. I'm more like your junior high science teacher introducing you to your first telescope.

What follows is simply a summary of what was written in the last letter amplified with some new insights. When I look at our history with God through the Prism of Humility and Gratitude, I see the following:

1. Nothingness
2. This Present Life: A Profound Gift
3. Heaven: Having Everything Forever

There was a time when we were not. No body, soul, and spirit. No consciousness. No mind, will, and emotions. Then a kind of Big Bang happened. We began to exist and were given the profound and incomprehensible gift of life. If life is not a gift then why do we fight so hard to sustain it and why do we mourn when someone commits suicide in the prime of life?

An acquaintance who is an atheist recently asked me, "Aaron, after all that you've been through, how can you still claim that life is a wonderful gift?" Without him having the framework of Christian redemption, I knew all my thoughts would be difficult to explain but I tried anyway.

"Life, I think," I began, wondering how I was going to make this palatable for this hidebound skeptic, "is made up of three kinds of gifts: pleasant gifts, neutral gifts, and painful gifts. I'm grateful for pleasant gifts because...well...they're pleasant. A good meal, a good book, the love of good friends, a successful fishing trip. Neutral gifts are neither pleasant nor painful but I'm grateful for them because they're *not* painful.

"Yes, I react to painful gifts like everyone else. I'd rather, in my natural inclinations, have my life made up of all pleasant gifts or at least a mix of pleasant and neutral gifts. But then I started to notice something: most of the healing, encouragement, and redemption that flows from one person to another emerges in the aftermath of a painful gift. We heal others, by God's grace, through our scars. This is what the late Catholic priest and writer Henri Nouwen called being a 'wounded healer.'

"Take my second cousin who lives in Montana. She enjoys the pleasant gifts of playing tennis, the encouragement of her woman's Bible study, and visiting her family in Maine, but most of the healing and encouragement that has come through her to other people has come through her scars. She struggled with depression and anxiety for years. When I first moved to Fawn Creek, during some of my darkest days, I received brief letters from her that really helped. Put in Christian terms, Christ was encouraging me through her."

"Aaron, I agree with everything you've said," he responded, "except the God talk. I do think human beings encourage each other but it doesn't have anything to do with God. It's a mechanism of evolution that helps the species survive." And with that we both reached an agreement and an impasse that wasn't going to be bridged in one evening.

Study Group, during this profound gift we call life, you and I have experienced a second spiritual Big Bang. Just as we went from nothingness to physical existence in the second Big Bang, as Christians, we go from mere physical existence to a dynamic, new spiritual existence. The Bible describes this using a variety of words: regeneration, redemption, justification, becoming a new creation, being born again, forgiveness of sins, the gift of eternal life, etc. In fact, for the Christian, this life is comprised of four kinds of gifts: pleasant gifts, neutral gifts, painful gifts, and the Gift of Eternal Life. The last one is the greatest. It begins in this life and reverberates into the next. In this life, we get the down payment, in the next we will be paid in full. In this life, we get the engagement ring, in the next we will be a Bride in a glorious marriage ceremony. In this life, we get the appetizers and salad, in the next we will feast on an endless banquet of exquisite fare.

In heaven, we will have the Beatific Vision and an unimaginable unity and fullness with the Father, Son, and Holy Spirit in the presence of heavenly creatures and an innumerable company of angels. The Beauty, Goodness, and Truth we see in this life are mere shadows compared to the boundless reality of those transcendental virtues in the life to come. Eye hasn't seen, nor ear heard, nor has entered into the mind of man what God has prepared for them that love Him. To distill it one sentence: In heaven we get everything forever.

Our history with God then can be summed up as follows: We go from nothingness to getting everything forever and receive the profound gift of life (physical and spiritual) in between. This epiphany should create a prism of humility and gratitude through which we see our sojourn here on earth. This prism will greatly help you on your journey to the gold rush.

Gratitude is the offspring of humility. Humility acknowledges that we are nothing without God; gratitude gives thanks for everything we receive beyond nothing: physical existence and its gifts (pleasant, neutral, and painful) and the gift of eternal life that is inaugurated in this life and is fulfilled in heaven where we receive everything forever. Gratitude and humility are not one-time events but are disciplines that need to be regularly practiced. That's why your grandmother emphasized the importance of counting your blessings.

If we are journeying from New York City to northern California for the gold rush of 1849, having gratitude and humility dominant in our lives is like having two divisions of Union soldiers along for the journey. That's 24,000 soldiers providing protection, provision, wisdom, and guidance as our wagon train heads west. If bandits, outlaws, unfriendly Indians, wild animals, inclement weather, and scarcity of water (the world, the flesh, and the devil) try to afflict us, we will still make it to the gold rush ("Well done, you good and faithful servant"). The world, the flesh, and the devil tempt us to see the journey through the lens of entitlement, ingratitude, and victimhood rather than the prism of humility, gratitude, and victory.

If we have an unbroken series of pleasant gifts, the world, the flesh, and the devil will try to entice us with pride and complacency. In contrast, humility and gratitude will constantly remind us that we are nothing without God and that every good gift comes down from the Father of Lights (James 1:16–18).

If we encounter adversity and trauma, humility and gratitude will try to lead us on a journey where we realize that our scars are painful gifts and that the redemptive workings of God through us to others come mostly through these scars. Everything humility and gratitude try to teach us, the world, the flesh, and the devil will try to teach the opposite.

Previous letters have chronicled this journey. It is mysterious and not formulaic, though some common elements emerge. Humility teaches us to have our expectations congruent with a fallen world that is also a "soul-making" world. There may be disappointment and "having it out with God" or even a grieving process to endure but your process will probably look somewhat different than your neighbor's. You may find God in your ache or feel far away from God for a season. But, dear Study Group, here is what I want you to take away from this discussion: If you see the adversity and affliction you've been through more and more as painful gifts, and, if you see yourself more and more as a "wounded healer," you're on the right track and surely humility and gratitude have been your guides. If your life is instead marked by entitlement, ingratitude, offense, and bitterness, then the world, the flesh, and the devil have been your guides.

Perhaps my imagination is a bit fanciful but I believe that where humility and gratitude are our guides, heaven delights in our wounded healer status and laughs at the futility of the devil and his cohorts. They're like a boxer who can't land a clean punch or like Hall of Fame slugger Willie Stargell commenting on the difficulty of hitting the pitching of Sandy Koufax: "It's like trying to drink coffee with a fork." Again, they are like two divisions of Union soldiers creating both an impregnable defense and formidable offense against the enemies of the wagon train. The Nevada silver strike awaits you.

As a young Christian, I remember reading a book whose title escapes me at the moment but it was something like *Luminous Lives in Church History*. I no longer have it in my collection; it was one of many books I loaned out but was never returned. One chapter was called "The Face of Gratitude" and highlighted a Welsh woman (whose name also escapes me) who was prominent behind the scenes in the Welsh Revival of 1904–1905. She led a woman's prayer group whose fervent intercessions were instrumental in birthing the move of God. Her legacy may have begun with the revival but it came to full flower later in life when she became known by some of her admirers as "the face of gratitude."

In the decades that followed the Welsh Revival, she suffered what some of her friends would call "a double portion of affliction." She married young and had three sons but two were lost to influenza before their tenth birthday. After twenty years of marriage, her husband was killed in a boating accident in the prime of life. In middle age, she lost her hearing and lived in poverty or near poverty for several years until she moved in with her only surviving son who became a prominent pastor in Cardiff. As an elderly woman, she took a nasty spill down some icy outdoor stairway and was confined to a wheelchair for the rest of her life. She did live to see the birth of her first great-grandchild who was named after her late husband.

She said the ache of the loss of her two sons never really went away but she emerged grateful for the close relationship she had with the son who survived. She missed her husband terribly at times but gave thanks for twenty wonderful years. "Some marriages," she said, "don't even get one wonderful year." She lost her hearing but emphasized how wonderful it was to be able to see, touch, taste, and "smell the lilacs in spring." The upside of poverty she said was that it forced her to fast one day a week, and, being confined to a wheel chair was redemptive because it forced her to return to the fervent prayer life of her youth at the time of the Welsh Revival. She said that "in a wheelchair, you are a captive audience for God. Often there's nothing to do but pray."

Those who knew her said she had a preternatural cheerfulness and genuine appreciation for the small pleasures in life—a cup of tea, an evening stroll, a visit from a friend. She used to tell people "Happy are the grateful" and "Life isn't always good but God is." At her funeral, her son claimed that "to spend any amount of time with her was to see the face of gratitude." Her happiness was infectious and it cheered many souls in the swamp of despair.

Study Group, I must admit that sometimes when I meet people like this I initially wonder if their gratitude is authentic. Platitudes sometimes abound in a Christian subculture. Those who have endured adversity sometimes manufacture the expected religious response rather than giving the real one.

Gratitude is such a rare quality that when we encounter it, we are often astonished even among religious folk. Jesus cleansed the ten lepers (Luke 17:11–19) but only one, a Samaritan, returned to thank him. Dennis Prager, on his radio show, illustrates this point in exploring the concept of the missing ceiling tile. The natural human inclination is to notice the one missing tile in the ceiling rather than see all the other tiles. Human beings tend to focus on what they don't have rather on what they do have.

This woman's own testimony convinced me that she had true gratitude. I don't remember it verbatim but it went something like this:

"Gratitude is a journey," she said, "and, for me, it was by no means an overnight journey. Initially, I recoiled at the calamities that befell me. The name Israel means 'struggle with God,' and, like Jacob, I wrestled with God. Like Job, I had a row with God. I made my complaints known concerning the disproportionate amount of suffering that came my way. Like Job, I thought I heard God say, 'Where were you when I laid the foundations of the world?' He was vindicated, I was humbled, and

I took comfort in the arms of an infinitely wise God. I never knew *why* all this trouble came my way but I learned to trust the One who allowed it to happen. This experience became the foundation that gratitude was built upon. It defused my resentment and bitterness. I started to count my blessings. There's always someone worse off than you and there's always someone you can encourage through the affliction you've endured."

Dear Study Group, in reviewing this woman's story, I can't help but think about the testimony of psychiatrist Viktor Frankl in his famous book, *Man's Search for Meaning*. During his time as a prisoner of war at Auschwitz, he observed that the Nazis sought to control every area of the prisoners' lives. However, Frankl noted that there was one area that the Nazis couldn't control: how the prisoners *responded* to the efforts to control them.

Often on the road to the gold rush, you will not always be able to control *what* happens to you—you will only be able to control *how* you respond to it. Think of the silkworm. It eats the mulberry leaves and then secretes a protein-like substance out of its head to form a cocoon that farmers will then harvest for silk, one of the finest fabrics in the world. Think of the mulberry leaves as what happens to us in this life—pleasant gifts, painful gifts, neutral gifts. If we respond to these gifts with gratitude and humility, we too can produce precious silk—love, joy, peace, patience, kindness, generosity, faithfulness, gentleness, and self-control (Galatians

5:22, 23)—and become a "face of gratitude" for the people in our lives.

Grace and peace to you.

Under the Tender Mercies,
Uncle Aaron

Dear Carson, Dennis, Alan, Paul, Bill, and John:

In thinking about our call to be wounded healers, I'm convinced that I could write several letters on the subject and their cumulative effect wouldn't be nearly as powerful as Thornton Wilder's one act play *The Angel that Troubled the Waters*. I have no commentary on the play; it speaks for itself.

The play is based on John 5:1—4 and dramatizes the story of the pool of Bethesda where healings take place whenever an angel stirs the water. A physician who struggles with melancholy periodically comes to the pool hoping to be healed of his depression. The angel finally comes to the pool when the doctor is there but blocks him from entering the pool and receiving healing. The dialogue then goes as follows:

Angel:	"Draw back, physician, this moment is not for you."
Physician:	"Angelic visitor, I pray thee, listen to my prayer."
Angel:	"Healing is not for you."
Physician:	"Surely, surely, the angels are wise. Surely, O Prince, you are not deceived by my apparent whole-

	ness. Your eyes can see the nets in which my nets are caught; the sin into which all my endeavors sink half—performed cannot be concealed from you."
Angel:	"I know."

Interlude

Physician:	"Oh, in such an hour I was born, and doubly fearful to me is the flaw in my heart. Must I drag my shame, Prince and Singer, all my days more bowed and broken than my neighbor?"
Angel:	"Without your wound where would your power be? It is your very sadness that makes your low voice tremble into the hearts of men. The very angels themselves cannot persuade the wretched and blundering children on earth as can one human being broken on the wheels of living. In Love's service only the wounded soldiers can serve. Draw back."

Later a person enters the pool first and is miraculously healed. In his good fortune, he turns to the physician and says, "Please come with me. It is only an hour to my home. My son is lost in dark thoughts. I do not understand him and only you have ever lifted his mood. Only an hour…There is also my daughter: since her child died, she sits in the shadow. She will not listen to us but she will listen to you."

Under the Tender Mercies,
Uncle Aaron

CHAPTER 20

Dear Carson, Dennis, Alan, Paul, Bill, and John:

A young man or woman could learn a lot by eavesdropping on three middle-aged men while they divulged their greatest regrets about their fleeting earthly sojourn. Karl Stonegaard, Father Hewitt, and I shared such an evening on Karl's last night over a steak dinner that was followed by excellent cigars on the back deck of my cabin.

A brilliant harvest moon rendered my outside deck light unnecessary and an Indian summer evening provided enough comfort so that three loquacious gents like us would be talking until midnight. A subdued Fawn Creek sang a mournful song not meant for those in the vigor of youth but for those who had learnt from the occasional foolishness of that vigor.

Common themes began to emerge as we watched Father Hewitt's perfect smoke rings ascend to the starry host. The importance of relationships was highlighted, underscored, and italicized. We all agreed that it's normal for men to want to achieve and build something outside of home and hearth. Karl and I groaned in unison and admitted that we had, for at least a season in our lives, sacrificed important relationships on the altar of achievement. All three of us knew men who sadly at the end of their lives possessed at least four things: financial security, numerous awards on their office wall, no friends, and a resentful wife. Karl spoke for all three of us when he said, "Except for the grace of God there go I."

Before the last cigar was extinguished around midnight, we all agreed that we didn't want to repeat the past sins of neglecting important relationships. While Karl and I confessed regrets related to marriage and family that were later, by the grace of God, resolved, Father Hewitt had second thoughts about his relationship to his younger brother, Sean, who left the Catholic Church during his college years.

"There were times when Sean really needed me," Father Hewitt began soberly, "and I wasn't there. In seminary and early in my priesthood it was all shoulder to the wheel and nose to the grindstone. I wasn't out to make a name for myself; I was just trying to keep up with a big workload. A once-a-week phone call may have made a difference, but, I'm not sure because Sean is, hands down, one of the most stubborn people you'll ever meet. At my mother's request I did start calling him more, but, by then, it was too late."

Carson, thanks for your most recent phone call. I was happy to hear you had good luck with walleye at Windham Lake as the season soon comes to a close. I never had much luck there but I did notice that the locals, who knew the lake well, landed some lunkers this time of the year using minnows and perch.

Congratulations on adding two members to your Study Group. It's a wise move to break the study up into two groups of four and I'm honored and delighted that all eight of you will get together every other month to read and discuss my letters. I rejoice that recent letters on humility and gratitude have opened up new spiritual vistas for the group. Perhaps my greatest qualification for writing these letters is because I am a "recovering whiner."

Speaking of letter-writing…just as in past books I've written, I've come to that juncture in the creative process where the Holy Spirit taps me on the shoulder and says, "Aaron, you're almost finished." My mind and emotions tell me that this is the stretch run. Where it ends exactly I'm not sure, but it will end soon. I'm open to future correspondence with the Study Group as the Holy Spirit directs. You've been a wonderful audience.

Previous letters have explored how Christians from different faith traditions have used "guides"—Scripture, Tradition, the Magisterium, the Holy Spirit, etc.—to lead them from Boston to the Nevada silver strike. What should be obvious by now is how certain spiritual luminaries (see the previous letter—"the face of gratitude") can serve as guides or a spiritual GPS to the place of hearing "Well done, you good and faithful servant." They have a certain quality of being, a certain ontological excellence that we identify as Christ-likeness, saintliness, or godliness. If we have wandered from the true path and are, for example, squatting at Bitter Creek in the Valley of Resentment, encountering such a person can serve as a corrective and help us get back on the road to the gold rush. We follow them as they follow Christ. We behold Christ in them and are transformed. Dear Study Group, may the eyes of your heart be enlightened to recognize these people when they enter your life.

A fitting title to describe the summer between my second and third year of seminary would be "A Tale of Two Churches." As someone who wanted to be the senior pastor of a church someday, I used that summer to visit different churches in town in order to find a model for the kind of church I wanted to shepherd. Initially, there was an unnamed church in an unnamed suburb that had me, for at least most of that summer, seeing stars.

There was no doubt God was blessing this church. With a beautiful brick building, a growing congregation, and a burgeoning budget, this church became exemplary for our denomination. An eloquent pastor used solid exegesis and effective storytelling to help his audience with their daily challenges. A gifted worship leader and skilled musicians made the contemporary worship service the talk of the denomination. And, yet, despite all the outward displays of success and giftedness, by the end of summer, an unidentified check in my spirit prohibited me from making this church the model for any future church I would pastor. It would be years later before I could understand this reticence and unpackage its meaning.

The autumn following that summer, an African American friend of mine at seminary invited me to attend the church where he was doing his internship. It was a multicultural church in the inner city made up mostly of the working poor and lower middle-class people with a sprinkling of middle-class folk and university students. After years of being in culturally homogeneous churches (middle-class, white), the diversity in this local church, especially as it manifested itself in the worship service, was refreshing. However, as a budding senior pastor, initially this congregation was not the model I was looking for.

When I attended this church for the first time, I assessed it through the lens of the "holy trinity" of church success—Building, Budget, and Attendance—and found it wanting. Dated and dilapidated, it seemed like the building needed a new everything: church sign, carpet, exterior and interior paint, furnace, windows, electrical fixtures, etc. A down economy meant families leaving the church to find work elsewhere. This caused a reduced church budget that almost forced the senior pastor, Tyrell Jefferson, to get a part-time job selling life insurance.

On Sunday mornings, I'd walk into a church with congregants numbering a little north of 130. Despite all the outward signs of struggle and misfortune, after the worship service and after the sermon, after the potluck and after the final goodbyes, driving home I felt like Jacob, forced to exclaim, "Surely God is in this place!" Just like the suburban church, it would be years later before I could understand and articulate the significance of this experience.

With the suburban church, it was obvious that God was blessing them in the areas of the "sacred triumvirate" of church success—Building, Budget, Attendance—but I never left their service feeling like

Jacob at Bethel: "Surely God is in this place!" (Genesis 28:16). With the urban church, it was obvious that they were struggling in these three areas, and yet, in the dozens of times I attended the church, I felt the unmistakable presence of God. Years later, Rick Joyner (no relation), of Morning Star Ministries, in his book *The Harvest*, would trenchantly sum up my experience by observing that God "will bless many things that He will not inhabit." Just because something's successful doesn't mean God's in it.

This is not to say that there weren't many wonderful people at the suburban church, but I noticed that, over the years, many of the outstanding souls I knew left the church. There was a different spiritual ethos at each church and it was directly related to the Pursuit of the One Thing.

To be fair, the pastor at the suburban church was not a bad man and there was truth in the message he communicated: An earnest application of the principles of the Christian faith can benefit your life in the areas of marriage, family, work, finances, etc. The problem here, as I've mentioned in other letters, is that God becomes a means to an end. In this utilitarian relationship, the end is not an intimate relationship with the Father, Son, and Holy Spirit, but a blessed life as the result of integrating the Judeo-Christian value system into the important areas of human existence. The parishioner then becomes more intimate with a value system than Christ himself. An additional problem with the ethos of this church was that their definition of the blessed life was wedded to some of the more negative aspects of the American Dream. To his credit, the senior pastor, in his teaching ministry, avoided egregious materialism, but it was obvious that the Christian life had been defined as the pursuit of a blessed life within the socioeconomic context of an affluent suburb.

Study Group, this comes as a revelation to some people but covetousness doesn't distinguish among the classes. Poor people can prostrate themselves before the idol of consumerism and materialism just as much as the rich and middle-class. However, at the inner city church I attended, many lived near or at the poverty-line, but were, as the New Testament says, "Rich towards God." Senior pastor, Tyrell Jefferson, opined one Sunday that, "Sometimes it's easier for poor folk to keep Jesus front and center, to make him the alpha and omega, because Jesus, along with their family and friends, is all they have."

This dynamic along with the leadership of Pastor Jefferson resulted in preaching, teaching, worship, fellowship, evangelism, and social ministry that magnified Christ. At the suburban church, there was a tacit invitation to utilize biblical principles in the pursuit of a blessed life in an affluent suburb. At the inner city church, there was a clarion call to the Pursuit of the One Thing. The first was an invitation to seek a certain kind of life; the second was an exhortation to pursue a certain kind of relationship. I ran from the former and to the latter and continued to have a relationship with Pastor Jefferson and his flock for years to come.

Earlier in this letter, I mentioned the importance of spiritual luminaries—believers with a unique quality of being that are often described as Christ-like, godly, or saintly—and their role as corrective guides on the road to the gold rush. They are like a tuning fork for the various instruments in the orchestra we call the human being.

The human being is an anthropological orchestra. Body, soul, and spirit. Mind, will, and emotions. A multilayered being with great complexity and a heart that the prophet Jeremiah described as deceitful and full of twists and turns (Jeremiah 17:9). When the pure and true tone of the tuning fork is struck, all the other instruments in the orchestra must adjust themselves to match the fork's consistent tone. For a season, I was seduced by the outward success of the suburban church. Many of my instruments went out of tune, but the spiritual tuning fork of Pastor Jefferson and his flock helped me become of one accord with the sublime tone called the Pursuit of the One Thing.

Dear Study Group, please understand how important it is early in your journey to choose the right tuning forks. What a different person I'd be right now had I made (and continued to make) the suburban church my tuning fork! Like the church itself, I'd probably be blessed but not inhabited. Instead of being on the road to Idaho silver strike, I'd be sequestered in the Desert of False Success. Not being inhabited doesn't mean eternal damnation, but instead describes a misguided Christian faith lacking the manifest presence of God.

Dear Study Group, please understand how important it is early in your journey to have the correct view of success. Without it you will probably end up in the

Desert of False Success. In high school, I knew a devout evangelical who would eventually become a millionaire in the import-export business. In my mind, he was a success in high school when he was bagging groceries at his uncle's grocery store and he is a success now. Why? Because both then and now he is doing God's will in pursuing the One Thing.

Mother Theresa of Calcutta said, "We are called to be faithful, not successful…" Let this sound wisdom be a tuning fork for you in a world of moral cacophony that often promotes a false concept of success.

Study Group, just as we need to be tuned-up by spiritual luminaries from time to time, we also need to become, by the grace of God, tuning forks ourselves. Rather than conclude with my own thoughts on this topic, I've taken the liberty of transcribing excerpts of a popular sermon by my mentor, the late Conrad Kersten, called "The Importance of the Small Things." He delivered this sermon at a major conference shortly before he retired. This makes for a rather long letter but your patience will be rewarded. The sermon will also show you where I've borrowed from him certain analogies and illustrations:

> …Now one of the things we hear today in popular culture through books and other media is "Don't sweat the little stuff." I find it interesting that in my life, after several years of marriage, family, ministry, and life experience in general, I see the utter importance of paying attention to the small things. Small things really matter in many areas of life. Now as far as the message of

popular culture and my opinion, in many ways, I think we're both right...

In the arena of human relationships I've definitely had to learn to not sweat the little stuff... When my two sons were teen-agers, they liked to listen to certain musical groups that I would never listen to if guided by my own taste in music. Once I realized the music wouldn't pollute their souls, I allowed it in our home. Don't sweat the little stuff...

In other precincts of life, it's very important to pay attention to the small things. One day, while listening to the Dennis Prager Show on the radio, Dennis had a guest who is a psychiatrist named Dr. Steven Marmer. What Dr. Marmer emphasized for that hour-long segment was how much of our happiness is made up of small pleasures. People often make the mistake of depending on big things to make them happy...

"I'll be happy when I finally get married and have a family." "I'll be happy when I move out of this lousy apartment and buy my first home." "I'll be happy when I get the promotion at work or the big pay raise..." If you're waiting around for the big things to make you happy, you'll miss all the small pleasures that could make you happy in the present...

And so many of these small pleasures are free! So many of my generation remember being a boy and playing all day in the woods by their home with neighborhood friends. We'd play cowboys and Indians or maybe spend the entire day building a fort. A nearby pond could mesmerize us for hours with tadpoles, frogs, salamanders, and different waterfowl. Life was full of wonder and the only price tag was the physical exhaustion we felt at the end of the day.

Even now, as a seasoned citizen, the lion's share of my happiness is rooted in the small pleasures. The cup of coffee to start my day and then my morning devotions. Sometimes while studying the Scripture, an insight from some scholar will break a passage wide open. Then my morning paper and first things first: a quick peek at the baseball box scores. This boy from Michigan needs to know how his Tigers are doing. A morning walk through a nearby park with my beloved wife, Ruth. Later at lunch, I meet a good friend at a restaurant that has the best barbequed chicken and baked beans. My day continues with small pleasure after small pleasure until I crawl into bed at night with an excellent book by David McCullough about the building of the Panama Canal while Ruth reads a novel by Agatha Christie.

Dear listener, just as small pleasures are often overlooked as the source of much of our happiness, small decisions are often overlooked in who we become as people. We become our decisions and life is made up of mostly of small decisions.

All Christians can relate to how major decisions related to major issues can produce major changes in people's lives. For example, a young couple gets married in their early twenties and experience tension in their relationship because both have significant levels of selfishness in their lives. Then the wife gets pregnant and gives birth to a baby boy. He has Down's syndrome. Both the parents retreat from their past narcissism and make significant sacrifices of time, energy, and money for the child. Over the years, they are both transformed into other-centered, generous people. They insist what a gift their son has been to the family and how he has taught them so much more than they have taught him.

Most people don't have a major challenge like this. Their lives are made up of small decisions, many that they're not even aware they're making. This lack of awareness can wreak havoc in their lives. Like Gulliver, they are asleep when the little people tied them down and secured them with many small pieces of thread…

A husband and wife I knew had a pretty good marriage ten years after walking down the aisle. Like many marriages they needed some fine-tuning but they were headed in the right direction and were happier than most couples. Then the husband started to make some small decisions and the cumulative effect of those decisions had harmful consequences for their marriage. I call it the Gulliver Effect. Many small decisions like many pieces of thread can paralyze a blessed union. Some people may also call this "death by a thousand small cuts."

The husband was up for a big promotion at work. He was already doing excellent work but wanted to go beyond excellent in order to come out on top. As a result of this, he began to give his wife and kids what I call a "negative tithe."

A negative tithe is when you give 10 percent less than usual to several important areas of your life. The net effect is significant damage to relationships.

We'll call the husband "Phil," though that is not his real name. Phil started to spend about 10 percent more time at work and took more work home with him. Yes, you guessed it, he spent about 10 percent more time than usual doing work-related tasks at home. He began to spend about 10 percent less time with his wife after work talking about their day over wine, cheese, and crackers, and 10 percent more time alone in front of the TV. He spent about 10 percent less time with his two small children and 10 percent less time helping with jobs around the house. He was 10 percent less involved with his church and spiritual life.

Now, I'm not sure that all these things were 10 percent. I'm simply trying to make the point that Phil made small, subtle decisions. Phil's wife was a real trooper, and put up with it for awhile, but eventually she came into my office alone and broke down crying:

"Something's really wrong with my marriage, Pastor Kersten. I can't put my finger on it. Phil's not involved in some gross sin. He's not cheating on me. He doesn't have a secret addiction. He's not bankrupting our finances. It feels like a lot of small things. Emotionally I feel I'm getting nickled and dimed to death."

Fortunately, dear audience, this story has a happy ending. No, Phil didn't get the promotion. He fell victim to office politics. He didn't get the promotion but he woke up about his marriage and family. For a season, he neglected his wife and kids, but he didn't become a neglectful husband. He spent a little time in the doghouse and deserved it, but now their marriage is better than ever.

Now, the good news is that small decisions can go in the other direction and have the anti-Gulliver Effect. The cumulative effect of those decisions over a lifetime can produce a soul who is conformed to the image of Christ. A soul that looks like Christ…

My first pastorate had every trial imaginable. In our minds, we all have a list of stereotypical church conflicts that could happen. Well, they *all* happened at my first church and I have the emotional scar tissue to prove it. Now, when a young pastor finds himself in such adversity, his first instinct is to look for people in the church who can be a refuge of sanity amidst the insanity. I found such people in two retired couples who have long since gone on to their reward…

What struck me most initially about these two couples was how ordinary they were in every way except they had an extraordinary quality of being, a Christ-likeness that was obvious for anyone who had eyes to see and ears to hear. Their lives had definitely been salted and peppered by different trials, probably more than the average Christian. But there were no major dramas in their biographies. No Down syndrome children, no spouses with terminal cancer, no decade-long financial crisis.

"Usually, Christian growth isn't about the big things," I overheard one of them say to a young couple at church. "Now, granted, a major trial or crisis can change your life in a big way. But, for many Christians, most of their growth comes by doing the little things over a long period of time."

About a week after overhearing this wise observation, I had a vision or mental picture while studying John 12:24 in preparing for a sermon: "Amen, amen, I say to you, unless a grain of wheat falls to the ground and dies, it remains just a grain of wheat; but if it dies, it produces much fruit."

Now, this wasn't a vision like you see in the Bible where Ezekiel sees spinning wheels or where the apostle John sees all kinds of supernatural visions in the Book of Revelation. It was more of a mental picture. I'd like to think of it as my sanctified imagination being influenced by the Holy Spirit but I'm not sure…

Instead of seeing a grain of wheat falling to the ground and dying, I saw four acorns fall off an oak tree, die, and become four large and beautiful oak trees that, in turn, produced more acorns. This represented the two couples and all the fruit in their lives. The small decisions they had made in their lives represented much of the death and rebirth that caused this transformation. Some of the small decisions I saw in the vision the couples actually made and some I saw I imagined they must have made. A small sampling of what was (probably) said and done:

He oversleeps but still squeezes in twenty minutes of prayer because he says, 'Something is better than nothing.' She's a little late for work but still waves and smiles at her retired neighbor who's sitting on his front porch reading the newspaper. He's also running a bit late for work but still lets two cars in his lane on the freeway who are merging from the right. She returns a subtle slight from a moody co-worker with a compliment. He is praised at work for a successful project and makes sure that a younger co-worker is honored for all the hard work he put into it. On the way home, she is patient at the grocery store checkout line even though it is taking four times longer because of a glitch with the cash register. He comes home and knows it's his turn to do the dirty dishes. After doing them, he wipes down the kitchen countertops too. An hour later, over beers and mixed nuts, they talk about their day but both husband and wife strive to listen a little more than talk.

The acorn falls into the ground and dies. In small increments over time, it becomes a big, beautiful oak tree. Dear audience, this should be exciting for you if you feel like an ordinary person who is living under the radar. Because of the cumulative effect of small decisions made over a long period of time, by the grace of God, you will wake up as an ordinary person with an extraordinary quality of being. You will wake up with the image and likeness of Christ! May the grace of God bless you and keep you during this transformation from acorn to full-grown oak tree. In Jesus name, amen.

Under the Tender Mercies,
Uncle Aaron

P.S: If you become an oak tree, you will also become a tuning fork.

CHAPTER 21

Dear Carson, Dennis, Alan, Paul, Bill, John, Jack, and Terry:

Here at Fawn Creek, the signs that autumn is coming to a close are fast upon us. Rusty orange needles are beginning to fall from the tamarack trees especially during the afternoon breeze. A distant mountain peak north of the Canadian border recently was dusted with snow after one of our colder nights. Lucy, my beloved Border Collie, knows that something is up. She must know that a big change is coming that will limit her movements because she is wearing my arm out with endless fetching of lime-green tennis balls. If this keeps up, I'll need Tommy John surgery! A few nights back, Father Hewitt and I probably had our last smoke until spring. The mid-level cigars tasted good after DeeAnne MacAndrew's excellent chicken and dumplings dinner.

Carson, as usual, I enjoyed your thoughtful letter that arrived a few days ago. Again, I'm delighted that you find my letters helpful and were touched by the excerpts from Conrad Kersten's sermon. It doesn't surprise me that you feel especially drawn to certain older folks in your congregation who have a palpable love that you detect in their countenance, gestures, and tone of voice. It sounds to me like you've found your own tuning forks, your own full-grown, majestic oak trees.

George Orwell said, "...At age fifty, every man has the face he deserves." There's a lot of truth in this statement. The seasoned citizens in your church that you are drawn to are older than fifty, but the cumulative effect of small decisions made over a lifetime have given them a face (a face they deserve) that is radiant with the love of God. These are the faces of saints, of Christ-like people. These are spiritual luminaries and their shining countenances can provide light on the path to the silver strike. They made small decisions to love over a lifetime and *became* love.

The fruit of the Spirit (Galatians 5:22, 23) you mentioned you saw in their lives—love, joy, peace, patience, kindness, generosity, faithfulness, gentleness, self-control—are merely different manifestations of love, the first attribute the apostle Paul lists. For example, the joy you see is merely an "exuberant love," their peace is actually "serene love", and the patience they possess is a "longsuffering love." And so on and so forth. Dear Study Group, please follow them as they follow Christ.

Perhaps it is fitting that just as autumn, the season characterized by harvest, is coming to a close, so also are my harvest of insights that have been passed on to you with fear and trembling. But just as autumn and harvest will return next year, so I also sense that this is not the last you will hear from me. By the grace of God, Carson's eccentric uncle has more gas left in the tank and will be more than willing to renew our correspondence as the occasion arises.

Pastor Tyrell Jefferson used to say, "Denial is not a river in Egypt," then proceed to impart some uncomfortable truths to his congregation. Early in my pastorate, I was accosted by reality and had to come out of denial. A conversation with a respected elder in our church precipitated the process.

"In so many ways," he began over breakfast at a local diner, "life couldn't be better. After some difficult early years, the marriage has never been better. Ditto for the sex life. I've got the career I've always wanted and am making good money. We've had a few rough patches with one of our boys but there's hope that he might soon be back on the straight and narrow. Relationships are good; I can't keep up with all the friends I have. My morning devotions aren't dynamic but they're substantive and 'steady as she goes.' I don't need fireworks. And yet, having said all this, with so many blessings, something still feels like it's missing. I can't help but go back to what I heard in Sunday school as a kid: We won't be completely satisfied until we are in heaven."

A few days after this conversation, I came across these words of wisdom from C. S. Lewis:

> Most people, if they had really learned to look into their own hearts, would know that they do want, and want acutely, something that cannot be had in this world. There are all sorts of things in this world that offer to give it to you, but they never quite keep their promise. The longings which arise in us when we first fall in love, or think of some foreign country, or first take up some subject that excites us, are longings which

> no marriage, no travel, no learning, can really satisfy. I am not now speaking of what would ordinarily be called unsuccessful marriages, or holidays, or learned careers. I am speaking of the best possible ones. There was something we grasped at, in that first moment of longing, which just fades away in the reality. I think everyone knows what I mean. The wife may be a good wife, and the hotels and scenery may have been excellent, and chemistry may be a very interesting job: but something has evaded us.
>
> *Mere Christianity*

Lewis goes on in the same book to echo Augustine in opining why some of our desires are not satisfied in this life:

> The Christian says, "Creatures are not born with desires unless satisfaction for those desires exists." A baby feels hunger: well, there is such a thing as food. A duckling wants to swim: well, there is such a thing as water. Men feel sexual desire: well, there is such a thing as sex. If I find in myself a desire which no experience in this world can satisfy, the most probable explanation is that I was made for another world.
>
> *Mere Christianity*

When I listened to my elder at the diner reflect on his experience, like a "good pastor," I nodded in agreement, but I drove home from there with a hollow feeling, the same feeling I always get when there is a vast gulf between the message I preach and the man I really am. Later that night, I thought I heard the Holy Spirit say to me, "Aaron, you give mental assent to the doctrine of heaven but you are carefully arranging your life as if you could achieve heaven in the here and now."

Whether the voice was the Holy Spirit or my own better self, I'm not sure, but the words were painfully true. Rather than being honest like my good elder in admitting that "something's missing," I was in denial. Instead, I would redouble my efforts to arrange my world in such a way as to eradicate the "something's missing" feeling. There was an unconscious agenda that the right marriage, the right sex life, the right career, the right friendships, the right children, the right hobbies, the right travel, etc., could fill every void. During this season in my life, I realized that there wasn't much difference between myself and the suburban church I criticized in the last letter who were using biblical principles to carefully arrange their lives in the socioeconomic context of an affluent suburb. The human heart is full of twists and turns: I ran from the suburban church but was, in many ways, like them.

Dear Study Group, a person may start out on a journey from Boston to the northern California gold rush of 1849, but if he thinks he will be perfectly happy "arranging his life" in Springfield, Missouri, he won't make it to the gold strike. Again, this is not about eternal damnation; it's about pursuing the One Thing and fulfilling our destiny in Christ. Making it to the gold rush just can't be one option among many; it's attainment must be nonnegotiable. Over the centuries, the spiritual luminaries of church history have been a heaven-obsessed people. All they wanted to hear was "Well done, you good and faithful servant." By God's grace, they were able to jettison the natural human tendency to arrange their lives, defer complete gratification in this life, and hope for the satisfaction of every desire in the next. Scripture was a tuning fork for them:

> Do not store up for yourselves treasures on earth, where moth and decay destroy, and thieves break in and steal. But store up treasures in heaven, where neither moth nor decay destroys, nor thieves break in and steal. For where your treasure is, there also will your heart be.
>
> Matthew 6: 19–21

The apostle Paul confirms the words of Christ by exhorting the believers to focus on the things of heaven and not on the things of the earth (Colossians 3:1–4). He reminds them that their citizenship is in heaven (Philippians 3:20) and that through the redemptive work of Christ, they are seated in heavenly places (Ephesians 2:6). The writer of the Letter to the Hebrews encourages his audience to imitate those in the Old Testament narrative who accounted themselves strangers and aliens on the earth and were seeking a "better homeland, a heavenly one" (Hebrews 11:13–16).

Dear Study Group, perhaps you don't struggle with these issues like I did at your age. The journey to the Klondike gold rush was hampered for me until I admitted that I had the "something's missing" feeling, that I was carefully arranging my life in such a way in order to eradicate that feeling, and that the God of Grace was my only hope for substituting my tendency to arrange my life with the virtue and hope in the hereafter. May the God of all Grace bring us all to the point where we say "Klondike or bust!" No settling for a comfortable life in Topeka, Kansas, or Greely, Colorado.

Adam and Eve lived in the perfection of Eden—a kind of heaven—but, because of their fall, they were banished from the Garden and had to live east of Eden. Reentry into the Garden was prohibited by cherubim who guarded the tree of life with a fiery, revolving sword (Genesis 3:24). Past letters have chronicled the foolish, human tendency to follow our hearts rather than heed divine sources of authority such as Scripture and Tradition. Following our hearts often leads us to try to bypass the cherubim in order to reenter Eden so that we can experience the full satisfaction of heaven. When I was carefully arranging my life in order to eliminate the "something's missing" feeling, this is exactly what I was trying to do.

It is futile to try to sneak by the cherubim; the glossy perfection of Eden eludes us. A friend of mine with a troubled marriage told me that one of the biggest tensions in his relationship with his wife is that "she can never leave well enough alone. Everything has to be perfect and the perfect is the enemy of the good. Unfortunately for me, that means that being a good husband is not good enough. No, I must be able to read her mind and know exactly what she wants on her birthday."

What precipitated my correspondence with the Study Group—i.e., Keith's illicit use of sex and drugs—is also an obvious example. The goal is to attain some heightened or ecstatic state, a kind of erotic and pharmacological Eden that will hoodwink the angelic guardians. What's achieved instead is a "faux transcendence" with a huge price tag: the hollowing out of one's soul. All idolatry is merely an over-attachment to some created thing (e.g., money, sex, power, etc.) with the goal of achieving some inner fulfillment that will make the "something's missing" feeling go away.

Individuals are not the only ones who try to plunder the treasures of Eden; governments also do it. Think of the atheistic communist governments of the twentieth century with dictators (e.g., Stalin) who pursued some "workers' paradise" of the equal distribution of goods. "From each according to his abilities, to each according to his needs," Karl Marx said. Tragically, the more they pursued their utopian dreams, the more blood was shed with estimates as high as one hundred million lives when you factor in Mao's Communist China, Pol Pot's Cambodia, et al.

Secular people are not the only ones who try to achieve heaven on earth; religious people also try to fool the cherubim. I believe that the supernatural workings of God in healings, miracles, etc., did not end with the Acts of the Apostles (A.D. 62). However, I have met some Christians who seem to expect God to do things like this almost everyday. It's a "heaven now" kind of theology that overlooks the fact that the Book of the Acts of the Apostles recounts a history of the early church that took place over three decades, not three months. The supernatural wasn't happening everyday.

It should be obvious that the examples I've furnished are not all morally equivalent. The point is to highlight the futility of trying to reenter Eden. The sooner we admit we're tired of tangling with the cherubim, the sooner we can put our hope in heaven and head down the road to the Idaho silver strike. I have more to say on the subject of heaven but need to go to Clayton for a couple of days to visit friends and run some errands.

Grace and peace to you.

Under the Tender Mercies,
Uncle Aaron

CHAPTER 22

Dear Carson, Dennis, Alan, Paul, Bill, John, Jack, and Terry:

A light snow is falling here at Fawn Creek, but, according to the weather report, it should be all melted and gone by late afternoon. Jim McAndrew dropped off a load of firewood yesterday along with half a French apple pie from DeAnne. I helped him stack the wood under my deck and listened to him play amateur meteorologist in predicting a mild winter with below average snowfall. He made a convincing case and his memory of past winters at Fawn Creek is almost encyclopedic.

My two days in Clayton were uneventful and that's the way I like it, because, most of the time, no news is good news. A couple who is out of town opened their home to me. I fed their fat Tabby cat named Murphy, watered their plants, and kept a fire going most of the time. My second night I took Father Hewitt and another friend out to eat at the Mexican restaurant in town. Half of the evening was spent debating whether there really was any hope for the Mariners and Seahawks and then we moved on to weightier topics such as why wisdom comes through suffering. When Father Hewitt snatched the bill from the startled waitress at the end of the meal, he opined that "It's my turn to do a little suffering."

If you came away from the last letter feeling bloodied and bruised by the cherubim, you're not alone. Coming out of denial and acknowledging the futility of reentering Eden is not a one-time event that will, for a lifetime, immunize you from future folly. As someone who has, over the years, served as an occasional "spiritual piñata" for the cherubim, I know that such confessions need to be done over and over. But, at least, the last letter provides a good starting point for this one.

The Holy Spirit orchestrates epiphanies. The very same week I had the conversation with my elder at the diner about his "something's missing" feeling, a new member of our church came up to me after a Sunday morning service and said, "Pastor Joiner, I really appreciate your preaching and teaching. It's so down to earth and practical. I'm a bit tired of 'pie in the sky' sermons. Some pastors are so heavenly-minded they're no earthly good." Like a "good pastor," I smiled, thanked her, and asked her how long she had attended our church and where she lived before moving on and greeting the next person. The next morning, while feeling physically and emotionally spent over my second cup of coffee, I mused on this brief exchange, and, while half-agreeing with her, my thoughts were more occupied with rehabilitating the reputation of heaven, both with myself and those I served.

Again, C. S. Lewis is helpful here:

> If you read history you will find that the Christians who did most for the present world

> were just those who thought most of the next. The Apostles themselves, who set on foot the conversion of the Roman Empire, the great men who built up the Middle Ages, the English Evangelicals who abolished the Slave Trade, all left their mark on Earth, precisely because their minds were occupied with Heaven
>
> *Mere Christianity*

One could add to this list all the heavenly-minded Catholics who have led the way in building orphanages and hospitals all over the world; much of the leadership, including Martin Luther King, who marched in America for Civil Rights during the 1950s and 1960s; and, thirdly, many Christians who are out ahead in the arenas of charitable giving and volunteerism. If you are on the road from Philadelphia to the Yukon gold strike, a single-minded focus on the Yukon ("Well done, you good and faithful servant") doesn't preclude you from doing much good on the journey. In fact, you'll probably do more good with this focus than if you instead spent your energies arranging for a comfortable life in the City of Brotherly Love.

This will also sound counter-intuitive but the person with the single-minded focus on achieving the Yukon gold strike will probably, in general, be happier on his journey from Philadelphia to the Yukon than the person who stays in Philadelphia and pursues happiness with every fiber in his being. This assumes that all things are equal—i.e., the heavenly-minded soul is not being tortured in a North Korean prison while the earthly-minded person lives in the freedom of a comfortable middle-class lifestyle in Plymouth, Minnesota.

The woman who sets her affections on the heavens (Colossians 3:1) believes she won't get everything she wants in this life. As mentioned in previous letters, she knows she gets the appetizer and salad now, the main course and dessert later; the engagement ring now, the wedding later; the down payment now, the payment in full later; and glimpses of heaven now, the full reality of heaven later. Many of the settlers in Philadelphia will not defer the satisfaction of many of their desires and will want heaven now. Because their expectations of this life are not congruent with reality, they will experience more disappointment than the heavenly-minded and less happiness. Perhaps this is why Christians with high levels of engagement in their faith (e.g. church attendance, prayer, Bible study, engagement in the sacraments) in study after study, have significantly higher levels of happiness compared with secular people. See the excellent *Gross National Happiness* by Arthur Brooks for the factual basis of this claim.

Dear Study Group, please know that I'm not saying that completely secular, earthly-minded people cannot do much good and be happy while church-going folk can be unhappy and do much bad. I'm talking about *general tendencies.* On the topic of religious people outperforming secular people in the areas of charitable giving and volunteerism, see again Arthur Brooks in his seminal work *Who Really Cares?* On the relationship of the heavenly-minded to generosity, there are some helpful insights from the life of Abraham.

According to the writer of the Letter to the Hebrews, Abraham "was looking forward to the city with foundations, whose architect and maker is God" (Hebrews 11:10). In another passage, he is included in a constellation of saints who accounted themselves strangers and aliens on the earth and had a singular focus on a "better homeland, a heavenly one" (Hebrews 11:13–16). His pursuit of the heavenly city influenced his generosity in the here and now. He gave the priest Melchizedek, king of Salem, a tenth of everything he had (Genesis 14:20). When he and Lot parted ways, Abram (as he was called then) gave Lot a choice of which land he wanted for his flocks, herds, and tents. Lot chose the well-watered plains of Jordan (Genesis 13:1–11). Abraham could afford to be generous throughout his life because as the religious cliché says, "The world was not his home; he was just passing through." His attachment to material goods was comparable to a traveling businessman's attachment to the comforts and amenities of his hotel room. He may like the queen-size bed, cable television, and complimentary coffee, but he's not that emotionally invested in the room because he's just lodging there one night and it's not his real home.

One of the pleasures of attending St. Matthew's is all the big Catholic families I get to know. They pull into the church parking lot in their supersized vans and, if I'm lucky, they will sit in front of me and take up an entire pew. The Noonans, with their tribe of six boys and two girls, are such a family. Bob Noonan owns and operates a successful bakery and deli. Diane, his wife, is a homemaker and part-time cake decorator. They had me over for dinner one Saturday evening and I overheard an interesting conversation between Tommy, ten, and his brother Sammy, eight.

Sammy accused Tommy of eating the last piece of banana cream pie in the afternoon of that particular Saturday. He believed Tommy did it on purpose because he knew banana cream pie was Sammy's favorite and wanted to get under his skin. As the evening unfolded, Ben, eleven, confessed to eating the pie and Tommy was exonerated. Before Ben's confession, Tommy defended himself by saying, "Look, Sammy, banana cream pie isn't even one of my favorites. Besides, I knew Dad would be home from the bakery in a couple hours with pies and cakes just like he does every Saturday." There's a lesson here for those on the road to the gold rush: Why grasp and compete for that last piece of "pie" when our heavenly Father will give us all the "pies" and "cakes" we want in the next life—"desserts" that will never spoil or grow moldy? We can be generous here with our time, talent, and treasure because it will be restored many times over in the life to come.

Dear Study Group, my exhortation to you to seek a heavenly city whose builder and maker is God is not disconnected from the Pursuit of the One Thing. Christ is no longer in the flesh ministering in Palestine; he has been glorified and sits at the right hand of God in heaven. To behold him and pursue the One Thing *is* to fix your gaze on the heavenlies. The two cannot be separated.

Because of extreme adversity it is very difficult and even impossible for some people to be happy in this life. If you have an illness that causes you to experience constant excruciating pain, happiness will evade you. If you are the victim of a relationship involving frequent physical, emotional, and sexual abuse, happiness will be difficult to come by. To my knowledge, no one in the Study Group suffers from affliction like this; a certain level of happiness is an attainable goal for every one of us.

However, since we were created for heaven and the satisfaction of every desire, there is a significant gap between the happiness we achieve in this life and the longing for more emerging from our "Edenic DNA." The happiness we gain from the appetizer, salad, and bread sustains us but we still hunger for the main course and dessert. How we respond to this insatiability gap, this "something's missing" feeling, will determine if we make it to the gold rush. Again, this is not about eternal damnation but is about fulfilling our destiny in Christ and hearing "Well done, you good and faithful servant."

We can try to reenter Eden in this life and end up lost in the Mountains of Folly. We can give up on heaven completely, both in this life and in the life to come, and stagnate in the Desert of Apathy and Low Expectations. The spiritual luminaries of the past, in contrast, have trod a different path to the gold rush called the Living Hope. This Living Hope is a sturdy bridge that joins the here and now to the hereafter, who we are now to who we will be then, the measure of happiness we have now to the immeasurable bliss we will have in the life to come.

> Blessed be the God and Father of our Lord Jesus Christ, who in his great mercy gave us new birth to a living hope through the resurrection of Jesus Christ from the dead, to an inheritance that is imperishable, undefiled, and unfading, kept in heaven for you who by the power of God are safeguarded through faith, to a salvation that is ready to be revealed in the final time.
>
> 1 Peter 1:3–5

> See what love the Father has bestowed on us that we may be called the children of God. Yet so we are. The reason the world does not know us is that it did not know him. Beloved, we are God's children now; what we shall be has not yet been revealed. We do know that when it is revealed we shall be like him, for we shall see him as he is. Everyone who has this hope based on him makes himself pure, as he is pure."
>
> 1 John 3:1–3

The great souls who have walked on the Bridge of the Living Hope were willing to defer complete gratification until the next life. They put their hopeful expectation in Christ in the hereafter. When we endeavor, as I did, to arrange our lives in order to bridge the insatiability gap (the "Something's missing" feeling) and reenter Eden, there is an over-attachment to created things that is called idolatry. For example, early in my marriage with Claire, I subtly put pressure on her to bridge the insatiability gap in my life. People make lousy gods. Idolatry pollutes our souls but a hopeful expectation in Christ in the world to come *purifies* us from this pollution. With this hope in my life, Claire no longer had to meet every need because I knew some needs could only be met in heaven.

The Catechism of the Catholic Church echoes the witness of Scripture:

> The virtue of hope responds to the aspiration to happiness which God has placed in the heart of every man; it takes up the hopes which inspire men's activities and purifies them so as to order them to the Kingdom of heaven…
>
> *Catechism of the Catholic Church #1818*

My hope (no pun intended) is that in hopeful expectation of heaven, you will be like the saints who have gone before you: happy, generous, and eschewing idols on your journey to the city whose builder and architect is God.

And now, dear Study Group, my correspondence to you has come to a temporary close. Like the author of the Book of Ecclesiastes (e.g., "Fear God and keep his commandments"), I leave you with the summing up of my letters: Pursue the One Thing. Pursue intimacy with Christ and you will become like him and you will make him known. Truly, you will strike gold and hear "Well done, you good and faithful servant."

But grow in grace and in the knowledge of our Lord and Savior Jesus Christ. To him be glory now and to the day of eternity. [Amen]

2 Peter 3:18

Under the Tender Mercies,
Uncle Aaron

BIBLIOGRAPHY

Dear Carson, Dennis, Alan, Paul, Bill, John, Jack, and Terry:

There's an inch of snow on the ground and Thanksgiving is in three days. The Noonans have invited me and another bachelor from church, Wade Dickerson, to spend Thanksgiving with them. That's twelve people under one roof, many of whom are active young boys who like to roughhouse. Perhaps I can convince Wade, who is young and strong, to martyr himself in a free for all with the Noonan boys while I sample Bob Noonan's heavenly pies.

Carson told me over the phone that many in the group are interested in getting a list of books that I drew upon in my correspondence to you. It's difficult to recall every book, but here's a good beginning:

Athanasius, Saint. *Life of Antony*. Edited by Emilie Griffin. Translated by Robert C. Gregg. San Francisco: Harper San Francisco, 2006.

Augustine, Saint. *Confessions*. Introduction and Notes by Mark Vessey. Translated by Albert C. Outler. New York: Barnes and Noble Books: 2007.

Aurelius, Marcus. *The Meditations.* Translated by George Long. Amherst, NY: Prometheus Books, 1991.

Baker, Jeffrey. *John Keats and Symbolism.* New York: St. Martin's Press, 1986.

Brizendine, Louann. *The Male Brain.* New York: Broadway Books, 2010.

Brooks, Arthur. *Gross National Happiness: Why Happiness Matters for America-And How We Can Get More Of It.* New York: Basic Books, 2008.

—. *Who Really Cares: The Surprising Truth About Compassionate Conservatism.* New York: Basic Books, 2006.

Buechner, Frederick. *Wishful Thinking: A Theological ABC.* New York: Harper and Row, 1973.

Catechism of the Catholic Church. 2nd ed. Vatican City: Libreria Editrice Vaticana, 2000.

Caussade, Jean—Pierre de. *Abandonment to Divine Providence.* Mineola, NY: Dover Publications, 2008.

Conroy, Susan. *Mother Teresa, Lessons of Love and Secrets of Sanctity.* Huntington, IN: Our Sunday Visitor Publishing, 2003.

Crabb, Lawrence. *Finding God.* Grand Rapids, MI: Zondervan, 1993.

—. *Inside Out.* Colorado Springs, CO: NavPress, 1988.

—. *The Marriage Builder*. Grand Rapids, MI: Zondervan, 1992.

Dubay, Thomas. *Fire Within: St. Teresa of Avila, St. John of the Cross, and the Gospel on Prayer.* San Francisco: Ignatius Press, 1989.

Eldrege, John. *Wild at Heart*. Nashville: Thomas Nelson, 2002.

Frankl, Viktor. *Man's Search for Meaning*. Boston: Beacon Press, 2006.

Hick, John. *Evil and the God of Love*. London: Macmillan, 1977.

Joyner, Rick. *The Harvest*. New Kensington, PA: Whitaker House, 1993.

Kierkegaard, Soren. *Purity of Heart is to Will One Thing*. Blacksburg, VA: Blacksburg, VA: Wilder Publications, 2008.

Lewis, C.S. *The Business of Heaven.* Edited by Walter Hooper. San Diego: Harcourt Brace Jovanovich, 1984.

—. *Mere Christianity*. San Francisco: Harper San Francisco, 2001.

—. *The Screwtape Letters*. San Francisco: Harper San Francisco, 2001.

Milton, John. *Paradise Lost: Authoritative Text, Backgrounds, and Sources.* New York: Norton, 1993.

Nouwen, Henri. *The Wounded Healer.* New York: Random House, 1979.

Rutler, George William. *St. John Vianney: The Cure D'Ars Today*. San Francisco: Ignatius Press, 1988.

Shelden, Michael. *Orwell: The Authorized Biography*. New York: Harper Collins, 1991.

Spink, Kathryn. *Mother Teresa*: *A Complete Authorized Biography*. New York: Harper One, 2011.

Swann, Ingo. *The Great Apparitions of Mary: An Examination of Twenty—Two Supranormal Appearances.* New York: Crossroad, 1996.

Tugwell, Simon. *Ways of Imperfection*. London: Dartman, Longman, and Todd, 1984.

Vonderen Van, Jeff. *Families Where Grace is in Place*. Minneapolis: Bethany House, 2010.

Wilder, Thornton. *The Angel that Troubled the Waters and Other Plays by Thornton Wilder.* New York: Coward—McCann, 1928.